MOONLIGHT SHADOWS

Moonlight Shadows

by
Natalie Daniels

Dales Large Print Books
Long Preston, North Yorkshire,
England.

British Library Cataloguing in Publication Data.

Daniels, Natalie
    Moonlight shadows.

    A catalogue record for this book is
    available from the British Library

ISBN 1-85389-564-4 pbk

First published in Great Britain by Robert Hale Ltd., 1990

Published in Large Print July 1995 by arrangement with
Mrs Gillian White.

Dales Large Print is an imprint of
Library Magna Books Ltd.
Printed and bound in Great Britain by
T.J. Press (Padstow) Ltd., Cornwall, PL28 8RW.

One

She'd never been any good at games. In fact, during her middle school years she'd been nicknamed 'Barrel'. Now, years on, a slimmed-down version of Tara Conway went to make her excuses, much as she had done then.

There might have been some point, way back, in trying to make her exercise, not now. She was overcome by a wave of anger which served her frustration. It was all so undignified...

She knocked on the door and listened apprehensively for the deep 'Come in', ignoring the knowing smile on Wanda's face. Her old friend sat at the typewriter outside the managing director's office, feigning disinterest.

'Paul,' said Tara, inside the sanctum at last, efficient with her Filo-fax in one hand, her clipboard in the other, 'If I'm away next week there'll be nobody to chase up the Appleyard contract...we might even lose it.'

Paul Gilpin sat back in his chair and steamed out a sigh that left his shoulders sagging. 'You're your own worst enemy,' he said, removing his glasses and letting them swing round his finger, 'and you know it. Look what a difference this course made to Grahame...'

'I'm not Grahame and I'm doing OK without it.'

'I've spoken personally to Appleyards. They're signing tomorrow. Maurice is taking over that one until you get back. Heavens, Tara, we're only talking about a week of outward bound! Anyone would think we were forcing you to have your leg off! You're supposed to be looking forward to it...to be stimulated and excited by the challenge!'

Tara, who normally liked to hide herself under a sheen of super-sophistication and self-control, flopped down into the swivel chair on her side of the untidy desk and moaned. 'I thought I'd finished with this sort of mindless coercion when I left school. I notice you haven't put yourself forward to face this stimulating challenge of yours. It's all right for everyone else, but not for him at the top. Is that it?' A gold bangle jangled on a suntanned arm as Tara pushed back a tress of heavy brown hair. She raised her pointed chin aggressively, positioned herself in the chair and crossed her legs in front of her.

Paul laid his glasses gently down on top of a pile of papers. He had always been a little nervous of Tara without quite knowing why. He knew that others felt the same. She was too self-assured, he thought to himself, too unwilling to allow her doubts to show. Her image was too perfect. One day the mask was going to crack. It was hard for a woman executive, he supposed, and he understood her difficulties, but if only she could relax a bit more... He pressed his fingertips lightly together as if in prayer and surveyed Tara over the top. 'At fifty-five I doubt they'd take me,' he said. His voice changed from sleepy to sharp, his expression from bored to alert in a matter of seconds. 'You want to get on in this company?' he fired at her. 'You want to get to the top? You think because you've reached the higher echelons of the Imports Department in eight years the rest of your progress is going to be that easy, that fast?'

Paul, whose designer furniture company had grown ten times as fast in the last decade as in the whole previous twenty years of slogging, was more surprised at his success than anyone. It seemed, now, that nothing he touched could go wrong. His management team was the best. His salesmen were the best. His buyers were the best. Gilpins was still expanding. It had all suddenly come together and now his expertise and acumen were admired by everyone in the business. It was essential that his workforce remain in front and develop in every possible way. And in his eyes self-confidence, assertiveness and mental and physical fitness were a great part of the precious development of his future managers, as well as responsibility and trust...

Tara didn't see it at all in that way. She was competent, efficient and successful at a job she loved, and didn't understand why she should be shipped off to some inaccessible mountainside in North Wales in order to improve her performance. Apart from her natural abhorrence of such a venture, she was a little hurt that Paul should think she needed to go, although she would never have said so. She was fond of Paul, they all were. He was a person who cared about his employees, and no matter how big his company grew, he made sure he knew everyone who worked for him and used first-name terms.

'I think I've done well at Gilpins because I was lucky and came along at the right time, but also because I'm good at the job. I get along with people, and I know the kind of product you're looking for. Paul, I am not an adventurous, outdoor kind of person. I detest all sport, apart from the occasional knockabout game of tennis or a gentle swim in a warm pool. I am a cuddling-up-by-the-fire, listening-to-music-and-reading-a-book kind of person. Hell, I'm twenty-eight years old. I ought to know what sort of person I am by now, and I know that no rigorous, character-building outward bound course in Wales is going to make the slightest difference to me at all! The only result that's likely to come from it is that I'll return home a nervous wreck with a couple of broken legs... Come on, Paul, you know me well enough by now...'

He looked across his desk at her, at her perfectly sleek image. Petite, darkly attractive with those mahogany eyes, dark hair coiled on top of her head, she certainly was an asset to any company. And his customers liked her. 'Three times you've been in here with various excuses as to why it would be wrong for you to go...three times! First it was your mother...you couldn't leave her because she was getting married next month! Nonsense! One phone call to your mother and she told me she'd be relieved to get you out of her hair...you were too interfering! Then it was your flat...you had planned for the decorators to be in next week and didn't want to leave them. Fine! They were easily postponed for a week. Now we're getting nearer the truth, aren't we, now we've dealt with Appleyards? You clearly just don't want to go. Wouldn't it have been a lot easier if you hadn't wasted so much of my time and told me that in the first place?'

They say that people look like their dogs, and Paul added to the evidence. Kindly and likeable, but sharp as a needle, his chin was multi-layered and hung like that of James, his old English mastiff. Give him a problem and he'd nose around it and tear bits off it until he got down to the marrow. His hair, thin but sleek, parted in the centre of his head and fell, too long for his age, down past his ears. The bags under his eyes told of a troubled life, but the eyes themselves sparkled with a lively wit and a happiness that belied his natural hangdog expression. Now, though they were filled with sympathy for Tara's unhappy plight, there was humour in them, too.

'You're not going to change your mind, are you?' she said flatly.

Paul, known for his obstinacy, shook his head and raised his eyebrows, ready for another attack.

'And you're not going to tell me why, either, are you?'

He sounded tired when he replied. 'You know why.'

'Character building?'

He nodded slowly.

'Then there's nothing more to be said.' She got up stiffly, determined to let him see she was not merely annoyed, but openly hostile.

'Of course you might even enjoy it... once you get there...' His lips closed quickly after this last unfortunate remark, as if to stifle a laugh, and Tara closed the door behind her quietly and didn't deign to reply.

She drummed her carefully painted nails on the wheel of her navy-blue Morgan as she crept along the snarled-up A5, sucking in the fumes from the lorries. She wished she'd left the roof up. She'd stop and get a coffee and seal herself in...if this traffic would only keep moving so they got somewhere.

'Welcome to Wales.' Tara snorted. She glanced at her walking-boots on the floor of the passenger seat beside her...great, ugly things with bright red laces. They'd advised her to wear them in before she left. She hadn't had time. She'd only bought them yesterday. She'd never really believed it would come to this.

As far as the eye could see along the road that undulated before her, the traffic was stopped. Glass and bodywork glinted in sunshine. Tara was thirsty. She put the car out of gear yet again and pulled on the handbrake. Bored and uncomfortable she pulled out the course particulars from the flap on the top of her rucksack and grimaced once again. On the front of the glossy brochure was a picture of log cabins among pine-trees. Everything inside the rucksack was new, paid for by the company. Tara's city lifestyle didn't call for such items as waterproof jackets or trousers, thick, woollen socks, bobble hats, water-bottles, sets of pans and light tents!

'Supper' she read, 'seven-thirty, followed by introductions and coffee in the hall.' She moved the car ten feet along the road and started reading about tomorrow, Sunday.

Apparently they were going to walk some distance from the centre and spend the night camping, 'in order for us to quickly get to know each other', she read. She smiled at the familiarity in the wording...all cleverly designed for jolly togetherness, defences down! Well, she supposed she would survive. As Paul had said, it was only for a week. She could survive anything for a week, one way or another. As she'd discovered at school, there were always ways and means of avoiding the worst. Tara was a convincing liar! And she had this knee that tended to play up...

And Paul was right, Tara did try and make herself seem abler than she was. And it was a strain. No wonder she liked to stay in at night curled up in a chair with a book...it was only when she was on her own that she felt safe. Otherwise she put on an act...she had to convince people that she was efficient and capable and to do this she hid her vulnerability under that veneer of sophistication. It was hard carrying out such a high-powered job in a world of men...easier sometimes...but mostly much, much harder. Harder to be taken seriously...harder not to be pushed aside and spoken down to...harder not to be treated as someone whose behaviour, trying to be friendly, could be misinterpreted as something much more...

Only a few, well-chosen people knew the real Tara. Her mother, of course, was one, her friend Wanda was another...and then there had been Mathew...

Thank God the traffic was moving again. She checked the map and sighed as she realised how far she had to go. She'd be lucky if she got there by suppertime.

In some ways this was like going to boarding-school for the first time. Tara shivered as she remembered her mother's words, 'Run along and see if you can find some friends...' as if it was as easy as that, at seven, to make friends of those whispering, weaselly girls who all knew somebody else except her! But this wasn't as bad as that, not really. She was going here of her own free will. She wouldn't be away from home, miserable, for three months at a stretch. No-one could stop her leaving, no-one but herself, because she knew that if she left she would taste such bitter failure.

How she'd hated boarding-school. How she'd loathed games! It was hard to put on an act when you couldn't breathe properly and when the sweat was running down your back and when you were hopeless at running or catching a ball. And it was all done so publicly! But school-work had been quite different. You could bury yourself in your books, could sit quietly in the library, and then you were accepted by everybody except the few troublemakers who are always on the outside of the system. No wonder she'd done so well in her exams. No, it was physical things she was bad at...maybe that's why Mathew...

She turned right and the road cleared. She put her foot down and the car purred. She felt the wind lifting her hair and the sun became a friend again.

The brochure had been cleverly done. In reality the Outward Bound Centre was bleak. Yes, there were a few pine-trees, but not as many as there looked in the photograph. They looked...thinner somehow. And the photograph didn't show the grim mass of bare rock that provided the background to the chalets.

Built on poles off the ground, they looked, from here, more like chicken-huts. They would all have enjoyed a fresh coat of creosote.

Tara parked the Morgan, took a deep breath, and opened the door. She wrestled with her rucksack, and heaved her pigskin case out of the back, laying it down in the dust while she pulled up the car hood. All the while her eyes flicked over the other arrivals who talked in desultory groups round the door of the first hut under the rough-and-ready label 'Reception'.

Her mother's words, 'Run along and see if you can find some friends,' jangled in her brain and she had to concentrate to dismiss them.

Pretending to be intent on screwing down the roof, she watched as the party on the porch was joined by a posturing young man in shorts who, even from this distance, crackled with fitness. He was the sort of man she'd always disliked. Dark and swarthy, the crinkles at his eyes and the toughness of his skin made her think of an American Indian. So did the way his eyes glittered—fanaticism, she thought to herself—a keep-fit fanatic. She suspected he'd be a vegetarian.

Her high heels wobbled as she crossed the uneven ground carrying her rucksack and her case. The athletic-looking man was pointing to lists on the wooden door of the reception hut, so Tara went straight to read them, smiling automatically as her eyes met all those other ones.

Safely with her back to everyone else she leaned forward to see. Conway...she was first on the list, and she was in hut seven. God, it was like being a prisoner of war. She turned and unexpectedly faced the man in charge, his hand stretched towards her ready to shake. She put her rucksack down and gave her introductory smile.

'I'm Joe Cornel,' he said, with a flash of very white teeth. 'And you are...?'

'I'm Tara Conway,' she said. 'From Gilpins.'

'You've found your dormitory all right?' He nodded towards the lists. The man exuded energy!

Dormitory? She hadn't read anything about dormitories! Did he mean she was going to have to share a room with a chalet full of strangers? The smile, from years of practice, stayed on her face, and not a sign of her distress showed.

'My name is Joe Cornel,' he was saying again, loudly this time so that everyone could hear, 'and I'm in charge of this week's programme. It seems that most of you arrived some hours ago and so you probably know each other already. But those who don't, not to worry, we'll sort all that out this evening after supper. Might I suggest that now the majority are here you will go and unpack and sort yourselves out. There are fifty of you altogether on this management course, so you will be divided into groups for the activities. But for this evening we'll all stay together. If there's anything you need to know, any problems, you'll find me in chalet number one, which is the instructor's chalet, or at the reception here...'

Tara stopped listening. This was terrible. She was the only one in a dress. Her heels looked silly, so did her pigskin case. Obviously you were meant to stuff everything in your rucksack. How could she admit her car was crammed full of bits and pieces as well?

Most of the men had shorts on. The

20

majority of the few women did, too. The rest wore trousers. They all looked fit. They all looked the athletic type. Once again she cursed Paul for the way he was influenced by sales hype...this was clearly not the right sort of course for her, no, not at all. Just because Grahame Simpson had done well...

'Let me.'

'What?' Briefly she was taken off guard, and her feelings showed as she turned to the speaker.

'I said let me...take your case. And then we'll go back to your car and get the rest of your things. It's too hot for you to struggle with all this alone.'

'That's quite all right,' she said. 'I can manage. I was silly to bring so much in the first place.'

But he already had her case, and was swinging along beside her chatting in a relaxed and easy manner. 'Don't worry,' he said, squeezing up his eyes against the sunshine and moving uncomfortably near. 'It's not half as bad as you think it's going to be.'

'No?' she answered stiffly. 'And what makes you think I think that?'

'I just thought perhaps you weren't used

to this sort of thing.'

'Is anyone? Would anyone come here from choice?'

'Some do,' he said happily, missing the bite in her voice. 'You might even get to enjoy it.'

That was the second person who'd told her that. Tara bit her lip and gave him a weak smile. 'And why do you do it?' she asked, annoyed and discomforted by his familiarity. 'Why would a grown man come up here into the mountains and spend his life playing games? Or is your sideline trying to get off with the desperate women who are unfortunate enough to be sent here?'

She'd gone too far. He didn't deserve that! Why did she have to be so unpleasant when the man was trying to do her a favour?

Joe wasn't angry. Instead, his eyes lit up with surprised amusement. He didn't seem to care about the slight at all. But he dumped her bag in the gravel and winked.

'OK, you want to be left alone. I get the message. Fair enough. If you want any help, Miss Conway, just give me a call. Right?'

'Right,' she said primly, and staggered on feeling foolish. She longed to arrive at her designated chicken-hut to get her shoes off and take shelter from the swelteringly hot, early evening sun.

She was hungry, thirsty, hot and bad-tempered. She wanted a cool, foamy bath. But she wished she hadn't reacted to Joe Cornel in the way she had. She knew why without being told. She was frightened of him and his sort. She felt he was real and she was not, he found things easy while she didn't. He didn't have to struggle to be friendly and natural with people.

She got to the hut and opened the door. The wooden structure held the heat and it was no cooler inside than out. But worse than this was the sight of the ten beds, five each side, basic, metal beds with thin, distressed-looking mattresses. Not even made up, they stretched like the rungs of a ladder down the spartan wooden floor. Tara moved to the first one and threw her luggage down. She sat facing the door and removed her shoes.

She bent forward and rubbed her feet.

'Ten minutes 'til supper,' called a voice that reminded her of her games mistress. 'Ten minutes to freshen up and unpack...'

Tara thought the voice was addressing the room but it wasn't. It came from the next bed and was directed solely at her.

'You don't want to miss the food,' her neighbour went on encouragingly. 'You're going to need it over the next few days...energy...'

Slowly Tara raised her head, turned round and stared resignedly at the hearty speaker.

To all intents and purposes she was back at school, back in the situation she had hated so much at the time, but now there were no academic lessons to escape to, only sport, morning, noon and night, only sport...and a man who unnerved her so much she had lost her cool completely and behaved with the rudeness of a terrified child again.

Two

This was the end! They were to be assessed as the week went along—graded—and reports of their progress were to be sent to their various companies. Tara could see Paul's face now... But it wasn't funny. Her future with the firm might be influenced by her performance this week, and her work was her protection...

Joe Cornel strode out as casually as if the going was flat as Oxford Street. His bulging rucksack didn't appear to affect him. He pocketed his ordnance survey map, tucked his fingers in his shoulder straps and pressed on. The Happy Wanderer, Tara thought to herself, amused.

She couldn't help but like his smile... the V beside his eyes where the corners crinkled. The last time she'd been in the country she'd been with Mathew...She was glad she was in Joe's group. At school she was never in the group she wanted...hardly an asset to the team, she was never picked until last...

She'd woken up at six o'clock to darkness. Surely it wasn't time to get up yet? Words from last night's induction, words like co-operation and trust niggled her brain as the mattress buttons niggled her body. With the morning came memory, and with memory came dread. So this was day one...if she could get this over without mishap she was over the first hurdle.

Although she had had an early night, yesterday's journey had tired her. The meeting, she supposed, had been passable, she'd managed to talk and be pleasant. To watch her no-one would have guessed how hard it was. The sociable chit-chat might have gone better, she thought, if the organisers had considered providing a little alcohol instead of just that over-milky coffee.

Despite advice from the well-meaning Aileen, the girl with the games mistress voice, Tara had skipped breakfast. She'd opted instead for the extra half-hour in bed.

'You must eat,' insisted Aileen, reading out the day's instructions. 'We won't be stopping until eleven.' Eating, it seemed, was an important part of Aileen's life. And she was eager to include everyone else in her schedule.

Tucked up, bottomed out in the shape of the mattress, Tara had lain and watched as Aileen discarded her huge blue dressing-gown and donned her clothes for the day. 'Has anyone heard the forecast?' she called down the room. 'Do we know what the weather's going to do?' Nobody knew, so Aileen said, 'Best prepare for the worst then,' and pulled on track suit bottoms over gaberdine shorts, and thrust a second pair of socks into her pack. 'Can't be too careful,' she told a dozing Tara. 'Better be safe than sorry.'

When they'd gone for breakfast, Tara got up. She didn't possess a sensible pair of shorts, only brief ones for sunning in, so she chose a pair of jeans, a T-shirt and a sweat-shirt. Surely, if she took her rainproof clothing, although she didn't relish wearing it, she would be all right. She was prepared to do many things to keep her well-paid job, but not to appear ridiculous. Her hair she left loose, sweeping it from her face with a couple of combs.

'Tent,' she read off a list of what they would need for the trek. When she came to pick her rucksack up she could hardly

27

lift it. She emptied it and re-packed it, ignoring instructions and putting in only what she considered essential. Sleepily she wandered out into the ominously early morning sunshine, squeezing up her eyes against the brilliance.

'Provisions...collect your share from the cook-house on your way out,' Joe was saying. When she arrived his eyes rested on her for one long moment before he continued. 'Maps...everyone should have one, and I hope you've all remembered your compasses.' Tara hadn't, but she couldn't understand a compass so there wasn't much point in her having one.

'Right!' He was so organised! She smiled to herself. True to type, she thought, caught his eyes and gave a little frown. Unusual eyes...vividly blue for such a dark person...and again, like the rest of him, so full of energy!

He introduced the four instructors who were each to take a group. He sat on the porch to call out the names, waiting for a 'yes' from each individual as they understood. Tara wasn't concentrating. She was thinking of her mother who was about to do the wrong thing. Harry French was not the man for her. What was the need to marry anyway when you were her age? Couldn't they just enjoy each other with no strings attached?

'Tara Conway?'

She realised her name had been said several times, looked up and stared blankly into Joe Cornel's eyes.

'Tara Conway?'

'Yes?' Her voice sounded silly and small.

'Tara, you're in group A with me, all right?'

She nodded, annoyed that they felt they had to name the groups. It was all so silly! It was all so childish!

And then they were off, heading for the hills, obediently following the leader with their heads well down.

'I'm not used to this,' a young man with sandy hair fell in beside her. Tara was surprised.

'I thought I was the only one...'

'This isn't my cup of tea at all,' the young man puffed. 'Not at all.'

'That's funny. You look like the sort of person who plays squash!'

He laughed. 'Just goes to show how looks can deceive,' he told her. 'The only exercise I get is getting in and out of my car twice a day.'

29

'Well thank goodness I'm not alone,' Tara said. 'I thought I was.'

'We better stop talking,' said the young man desperately, 'or we'll never reach the top of this slope.'

'Everyone doing OK?' Joe called back over his shoulder. Neither of the backmarkers had the strength to reply. He waited at the top of the bluff until he was circled by all ten members of his group.

'We're going to take this steadily,' he explained. 'We don't want anyone overdoing it on the first day. just a steady pace with lots of pauses. If anyone feels like stopping they must say so.'

Never, thought Tara to herself. If it's the last thing I do I'll keep going. You don't have to wear shorts and have muscular, hairy legs to succeed in this. There's nothing to it...once you get a rhythm going.

She'd changed her tune by the time they scaled the second hill. Her breath caught in her throat and she longed for someone else to call a halt. Surprisingly, it was Aileen who shouted, 'Joe! Joe! Let's just stop a minute.'

'No problem.'

Tara looked at her watch and shook it.

Half an hour? Was that all? It felt as if they'd already been walking all morning. She looked back the way they'd come. The cars on the road below looked like dots. Her stomach rumbled and she felt faint. How long before they ate? What had Aileen told her? Eleven o'clock? She shook her watch again.

Jeremy and Simon, the two most extroverted males in the group, took the lead, and set a faster pace than Joe had done. The macho instructor dropped back and joined Tara and her slow friend, Pete.

'Managing?' he enquired, and Tara prickled with annoyance under her body heat.

'Don't worry about us,' she panted. 'We're not out to prove anything.'

'I'd noticed,' said Joe, looking cool and managing to speak quite normally. 'It levels out after this,' he said. 'No more climbing then. We're on the flat.'

Tara was too tired to feel relief. All her concentration was aimed at getting one leg to pass the other. Her back ached with the weight of the pack, and her right heel was on fire. If she'd been allowed to wear a pair of trainers, she was sure she would have coped better. The boots were so heavy, so uncomfortable. Joe stayed with them and Tara couldn't understand the ferocity of her irritation. Why did he affect her so? Why did he always stay cool, stay nice, whatever was happening? Did nothing rile him?

The breeze, which had begun pleasantly, became stronger. Soon her ears started to ache. She stopped, unhitched her rucksack, and took out her bobble hat. She couldn't endure earache on top of all the other discomforts no matter how silly she looked. She pulled it well down over her head. She was about to bend to take the weight of her infernal burden again when Joe picked it up as if it weighed nothing at all and helped her arms in.

He was laughing at her! There was no doubt in her mind! That must be what had annoyed her so! Amusement was written in every line of his face! She recognised it at last. Right...that was the last time she was going to accept his help. That was the last time she was going to stop for anything!

Tara found it helped to think of something else and try to forget what she was doing. In this way, she discovered, her body went into overdrive and her brain was left alone. It was just as painful, but less intensive. She cursed Paul and his silly training schemes over and over again. Neither her nor Pete had the strength for words, so they trudged along side by side at the rear of the group in silence, each wrapped in their own dark thoughts.

And Joe? What was he thinking? Did he get bored doing this same trek every week with a different group of up-and-coming executives? Did he scorn their unhealthy efforts? Did he laugh about them in hut number one with the other instructors when the day was finished? Tara was sure he must do.

When eleven o'clock came Tara, having given up hope long ago, felt she didn't need to stop. She could have gone on, mindlessly like this, until she dropped. It wasn't until she sat down that she felt the pain in her feet. It wasn't until she rested her arms that she felt the bruising.

'Here,' Joe was sitting next to her, undoing her pack and getting out her thermos flask. 'This'll make you feel better.' He poured her a cup of tea and she sat back and sipped it slowly. Only then did she notice the view.

'Oh! It's amazing! I've never been so

high up before! Look at the mountains rolling out in the distance. There's so much sky!'

'It's good isn't it?' said Joe, sipping his own tea and looking round to check that everyone was safely there. 'It's almost worth it.'

'I wouldn't go that far.' Tara noticed with horror that she was staring intently at his face. Yes,' she thought, as she quickly looked away. He could be an Indian, given a feathered head-dress and a dab of face paint. He's dark enough, muscular enough, fascinating enough... She stopped, disgusted with herself, and took her mind back to her mother's problems. Loneliness...that was the trouble...loneliness and fear of old age. It didn't matter that Tara reassured her, 'I'll be with you. We only live half an hour away from each other.' Tara's mother had said, 'You don't understand, that's not the same. I want someone of my own.'

'I am your own, aren't I?' Tara had asked, hurt.

'You'll find somebody one day, and then you won't want to be responsible for me...'

'Now you're just feeling sorry for yourself.'

'I'm not. I'm being realistic. And I'm fond of Harry.'

'But is fondness enough, Mum?' As if Tara had dealt satisfactorily with her own relationships!

Aileen brought her back to the present. She sidled up, munching a cheese roll. Tara remembered how hungry she was. 'That looks nice,' she said. 'I'm going to find mine.'

Hers had been squashed under the flask, but it tasted as good. She eased off her boots and her socks and surveyed her damaged heel.

'My God, you've blistered your blisters!' said Aileen, aghast. 'Joe ought to have a look at that.'

Tara tutted angrily. She felt she would hit Aileen if she went off to tell Joe. 'All it needs is a plaster.' But plasters was one of the items she had jettisoned in her economy drive back in the dormitory. 'I'm sorry, Aileen. I've left mine at the centre. Can I use one of yours?' Even this, Tara hated. Even having to ask for this much help was a problem. But she'd rather ask Aileen than have to go to Joe.

Aileen was in her element. 'I'll do it,' she said. 'Let me look. Hold it up.'

'What's the matter?'

Aileen made such a fuss that Joe noticed and came back from a conversation with somebody else.

'It's nothing.' Tara was immediately on the defensive.

'Let me see.'

'It's OK.' She felt her face reddening and cursed her tendency to blush.

'I said let me see.'

As he raised her heel with his cool hands she felt a tremor start at her foot and pulse through her body. 'I was just going to put a plaster on. It doesn't hurt.'

'It doesn't look as if it hurts,' he said, sarcastically. 'This needs more than a plaster, it wants a proper dressing.'

'There's no need...'

'There is a need if we're going to continue the trek and not be held up because of you.'

'Oh.' She was silently glum as he fetched his first-aid kit and expertly bandaged the raw place.

'Now, another pair of socks I think and then we'll ease this boot back on. This is obviously the first time you've worn them.'

'Yes it is.' Nothing was going to make

her pretend otherwise. She wanted to make it quite clear to Joe Cornel just what she thought of his pathetic expedition.

'Now try standing. Does that feel any better?'

It did. The pain had disappeared completely. She nodded and ventured a grateful smile. The one she got back sent her blood racing, her temples throbbing. There was something about him...he looked good up here in the mountains...there was a wildness that she couldn't name... She smiled again, but he missed it. He was gathering his flock together for the next gruelling phase.

'I thought this was meant to be a gentle trek.' Poor Pete would have liked a longer rest. He wasn't the only one. But the front runners had set off and Joe didn't want the party split.

'Two more hours and we'll stop for lunch. We'll stop for a good hour. You'll feel better, Pete, by then. All those muscles will have loosened up.'

'Oh that's what it is, the pain then? I thought it was my heart.'

'That's what it is. Believe me, it'll ease. But you'll be stiff in the morning.'

'That's what I like to hear,' said a

37

doleful Pete. 'Something to look forward to.'

In sympathy, Tara stayed with him, although she was already feeling a lot better than she had done at first. But if she was being completely honest she would have admitted it had nothing to do with her muscles, unless the muscles of the heart had anything to do with this. Her legs and her arms were still sore, but suddenly she could taste the mountain air, see the vivid colours. She was excited. She felt completely alive, and a new-found energy tumbled and coursed like a mountain waterfall through her veins.

Three

The place they stopped to camp for the night was barren and wild.

The jet-black pool was a perfect oval and set in a ring of crusty diamond mountains. Tara shuddered. No matter how hot she was she wouldn't swim in that! It was the kind of place where something unspeakable, something unearthly, skulked on the bottom...waiting...

But the two most intrepid male members of the group, Jeremy and Simon, were already stripping down to their pants, and horror screwed up Tara's face as she watched them break the surface of the dark water.

'I'd like to swim,' said Aileen, sweat streaking her ever-cheerful, willing face. 'But I bet it's freezing.'

'Feel it,' said Tara. 'I might wash in it later, but I'm not going in.'

Jeremy and Simon, following the map, had arrived at the allotted spot half an hour ago, and already their tents were neatly pitched. The grassy bank that fringed the lake was caked with sheep droppings, and Tara spent a disgusting ten minutes clearing a space for her brand-new, neatly-packed nylon shelter.

'Don't bother,' Joe said. 'Your ground-sheet will protect you from all that. It'll brush off easily in the morning.'

'I'm not spending the night rolling about on marbles of sheep dirt,' she told him, continuing doggedly with her task.

'The main thing is that you pick somewhere flat,' he commented, taking no notice of her aloofness. 'And the bit you've cleared slopes slightly.'

She ignored him and got out the instruction paper. 'Fig one,' she read silently, and stared in admiration at the agile stick person who seemed to have the ability to find the top and bottom of the flimsy material, and lay it out so it made sense.

Tara gave up, and sat for a while watching the efforts of the others. Aileen, whose tent appeared to be an old friend from her Guiding days, had no problem. She even had a pan of water boiling on her spindly-legged burner. She looked happily at home in this unsympathetic environment.

'Tea in a minute,' she beamed jovially at Tara, nodding a head of unruly blonde curls.

Tara wanted to ask Aileen for help, but couldn't. You didn't have to be a genius to erect a tent. She stared angrily at the paper again. She couldn't make head or tail of it. Her tent seemed to be different from everyone else's.

To look as if she was doing something, she laid out the pegs in neat rows. She watched the two swimmers splashing and playing in the water. She heard Aileen pour her tea. She noticed the content of the other group members as they collected wood for the fire. And she felt useless...useless, defeated and pathetic.

'Aileen,' she said, in a voice too sharp. 'I've never put up a tent before. Give me a hand...'

Once again, the pleasant, fresh-faced Aileen was pleased to be asked. In no time the tent was up and it seemed so simple.

Aileen was making tea for everyone in her capable way. Tara wanted to crawl into her comfortable-looking sleeping-bag and zip up the tent flap. This was exactly the sort of situation she hated. She knew she ought to be doing something—contributing in some way—but she didn't know how. And she feared, if she asked, she would be told to do something she couldn't. She could imagine how her report would read...lazy, unimaginative, surly...but she was none of those things!

Pete, sitting in front of his tent on the mucky grass rubbing his feet, didn't look too happy either. Tara picked up two cups of tea from the obliging Aileen and went over to join him.

'Sore?' she asked.

Pete nodded unhappily. 'I'd love to dip them in the water,' he said, 'but I just can't move that far at the moment. I've just got to sit for a bit...'

Tara understood. 'Hang on,' she said. 'I'll fetch a panful and you can dip your feet in one at a time.'

After he'd soothed them, she fetched dressings from Joe's first-aid box and wrapped them as she'd watched her own being treated. 'Better?'

'Oh, the relief.' And Pete sipped his tea and smiled for the first time.

'We're out of our depth, aren't we?' Tara declared. Pete agreed.

Joe was a blob on the far shore. He sat alone, fishing. As Tara watched he was joined by the other two girls in the group, Emma and Jenny. They sat beside him, close, interested. Tara tried to staunch the nagging feeling of jealousy that tightened her chest. What was this? Why on earth should she feel jealousy for someone she didn't know? Of course they would want to watch him fishing, help if they could. Of course they would.

She wouldn't have felt so badly about it if Emma hadn't been so stunningly attractive. Not only that, she was charming, lithe and athletic. just the sort of girl Joe would be attracted to. And here was she, moaning and groaning with swollen feet and a leaning tent...

God, she wished she was back home!

The four remaining men had a fire going. Tara smelled woodsmoke and felt sad. Woodsmoke reminded her of childhood, of autumn bonfires and Christmas. Woodsmoke reminded her of times with her father. He had died when she was seven...then she'd been sent to school.

The government paid for her to go so that her mother could work for the Ministry again. And they needed the money. But Tara had been so unhappy... Knowing that her mother needed to work, enjoyed working, she hadn't been able to write the letter she wanted: 'Please, please, take me away from this place. I am homesick, I am lonely, and I just want to come home.' Instead, she had insisted that she was fine, had carefully listed all the events of the day, had given no clue to her unhappiness.

And her marks were always so good that her mother never realised. It wasn't until only a few years ago that she had confessed to her mother her true unhappiness. 'I don't believe you!' Tara's mother had been appalled. 'And you never said. You never showed...'

'I couldn't, could I?' Tara had replied. 'But I always felt a bit betrayed. I felt you ought to have known!'

She'd felt better having said that. But it didn't take away the bad memories...the dread of the term beginning...the despairing feeling of packing that trunk...the stale smell of it...

And now woodsmoke. That smell of happier days.

They ate the fish with fresh brown rolls. They sat talking round the fire. Night came on skeletal black fingers that inched their way down the stark backbones of the mountains. When it got cold it was bitter. There was a safe warmth in their companionship. Tara felt a fondness spreading over her friends like a warm, brown rug.

They laughed. They talked with a familiarity they would never have used in more ordinary circumstances.

She watched the firelight playing across Joe's face, shining his blue-black hair. He was a muscular man of middle height, with strong shoulders and stocky legs. His face was firm and leathery. He wore red, and it suited him. She found his blue eyes disconcerting. They seemed to see so much without having to look. He was in his element here...relaxed, amusing and interesting. Even Tara began to calm down. Surprised, she realised she'd rarely experienced such a feeling of relaxed well-being. She was actually enjoying herself! She liked these strangers she was with! They were all, in various ways, dependent on one another in this hostile place, and she savoured the feeling this gave her. Just by being here, just by supporting everyone else, she was contributing...

Everyone went to bed except her and Joe, Simon and Jeremy. They were trying to talk man-talk, of journeys they had made, of climbs they had done. As they attempted to outdo each other it appeared that this week's activities were peanuts to them. Tara sat listening, willing the two men to go to bed and leave her alone with Joe. She blushed at the unexpectedness of her own thoughts. Why? Why did she want that? She had nothing to say to him. They had nothing in common. She despised his lifestyle as she was sure he would despise hers. Yet there was this chemistry...it was surely too strong for him not to be feeling it too. Go to bed, go to bed she willed her two irritatingly boring companions.

In a minute he would begin to wonder why she was hanging around. They all would. She was clearly uninterested in the conversation. She decided to say goodnight. She was in danger of making a fool of herself.

But she was half a second too late. 'I'm turning in,' said Jeremy, shivering. 'I want an early swim in the morning.'

You're mad, thought Tara. With sudden alarm she watched Simon get up to accompany him.

They sat together and listened to the low voices of the two men as they readied themselves for bed, said goodnight and zipped up their tents. They sat on, in silence, only hearing the crackling of the dying fire and the whispers of the wind as it sighed over the mountains. The pool, silent before, seemed to come alive in the dark night quiet, and tickled the shore with kisses.

Then their eyes met. They met and held for the longest moment Tara had ever experienced. And when Joe smiled, the gentle enquiry in it caused her beating heart to crush out all other sounds.

Slowly he got up and moved towards her, breaking the spell for an instant so that she felt frightened again. What was she doing? What on earth was she doing? But when she felt him there beside her, the electric force that passed between them cancelled out all thought.

He cupped her chin in his hand and brought her round to face him.

'Why are you smiling?' she asked.

'I didn't know I was,' he said.

'It's your eyes,' she told him softly, swallowing hard. 'They're always smiling. For a while I thought you were laughing at me, that you found me amusing because I was so bad at...'

He put his finger over her lips and she was silent. She hadn't wanted to talk anyway. There didn't seem the need for words just now.

Gently he brought his head towards her and there was total darkness as he blocked out the firelight. His lips covered hers and she tasted them...they were sweet as the mountain air, bitter as the night wind, and firm and forceful as the ruggedness all around them.

She lifted her hand to stroke his hair and was surprised at the coarseness of it. And then he pulled her close. She shivered as she wrapped herself in his warmth and felt the strength of his arms.

For a long while they sat there like that, still, like the mountains. The tremendous closeness she felt was more mental than physical. They communicated in the silence using words that were ageless.

'I don't think I'm ready for anything like this,' she said at last.

'What's wrong?' He spoke to her as if she were a baby.

'I'm afraid.'

'Yes. The power of it is frightening, isn't it?'

'Are you afraid?'

48

He laughed, and the small sound floated over the lake like a breeze. 'I'm always afraid.'

'You?' She pushed him away in surprise. 'You, who climbs mountains?'

'Yes, me who climbs mountains,' he said. 'Perhaps that's why I do it. To prove I'm not.'

'Who would you prove it to?'

'Myself.'

She thought about this. 'I just run away,' she told him.

'Or pretend you don't want to do it anyway,' he added for her.

'Yes.'

He kissed her a second time and she felt herself grow weightless. She was afraid he would absorb her completely and she would lose herself for ever in this place. She pulled back and he frowned. 'You're not going to run away from this,' he whispered. 'Not if I have anything to do with it.'

She looked away and stroked his hand, feeling the roughness of the skin, the soft contrast of the down on his arms.

'How do I know that you don't do this every week with somebody new,' she started to say.

'You just know,' he said. 'Don't use that as an excuse.'

She smiled and replied, 'You know me too well. It's strange...'

'You've been hurt,' he said. 'I can see that, too.'

'How?' she asked him.

'It's in your eyes.'

She screwed them up. 'I didn't know it showed.'

'It shows.'

They were silent again. Tara didn't want this experience ever to end. It was all too perfect. Something had to be wrong. She remembered feeling this way with Mathew once...until the time... It had taken her years to trust him. Now she remembered his anger, the look on his face, the words he had used. She frowned and Joe watched her. As naturally as if they had always been together like this, he rocked her gently and it was somehow comforting.

A week, Tara was thinking to herself. I can't get involved in a week. A game, something to take my mind off the hell of it all, that's all this will be. And she meant it. There was no possibility of Tara Conway getting involved with this charismatic stranger, no possibility of that at all. She'd learnt her lesson. She'd had her fingers burnt, and although she was questioning him, it was she who would do the betraying if there was any of that to be done.

But she showed nothing of these thoughts. Instead she returned his kisses, answered his whispers, and it was very late when they said a last goodnight and went to their tents.

Tara was uncomfortable. She kept sliding off the end of her bed-roll and pushing against the edge of the tent so it twisted and threatened to topple over and suffocate her. Every time she dropped off to sleep, she was jarred awake again. Thoughts of Joe got mixed with thoughts of Mathew and swirled round in bright kaleidoscopic colours. She tossed and turned, too hot, too tired, too confused.

In her dreams she pictured the gymnasium at Cranfield. It was so real she could smell wood and damp plimsolls. She could feel her own heart beating and it was her voice saying, 'I don't want to do it, Miss Coles. I've never been able to get over the horse. You know I haven't! I don't want to do it and I won't.'

And the horsy face of the red-haired

games mistress stared down at the fat child with ill-disguised contempt. 'Don't and can't and won't...not the sort of words I like to hear in my gym! Will and can and shall. Say those words after me, Tara Conway. Come on, let me hear you say those words. One way or another we'll make something of that body of yours whether or not I have to die in the attempt. Come on now! We've got a week to practise before the parents' day gym display. I want you vaulting over that horse like a bird by a week on Saturday. Come on! Repeat after me: will and can and shall...will and can and shall...'

And in her dreams she heard her own childish voice repeating those stinging words. And after that came the ripple of laughter from the class, a shower of icicles that turned her heart to water. Oh yes, Tara Conway, who had been a fat child, knew all about the unkindness of other people. Her body had let her down all those years ago, and it was something she was quite unable to forget.

Four

'I can't do it. I just can't do it! I know I can't.'

'You can, Tara, you can! just one more step then grab my hand!'

They were strangers again in the silver of the morning. By the time Tara woke, the rest of the party were packed and ready to go. Someone had offered her breakfast and she had sent them away not too politely.

'Leave me alone. Let me sleep. I've been awake all night,' she groaned.

A shower of rain in the night had soaked her boots. Unthinkingly, she had left them outside, not wanting the mucky things in the tent with her. Her socks had been stuffed inside them. She held them up now, bare foot sticking up in the air, crouched forward in order to put them on, and wrung the water from them.

'I've already lent you my second pair,' said Aileen in a worried voice. 'You'll have to ask Jenny or Emma.'

'Aileen,' Tara whined. 'Will you do it for me?'

Aileen was willing to help anybody, and now she gave Jenny a hand to undo her pack and find the elusive second pair of socks. Nobody berated Tara for not carrying a second pair of her own. They didn't have to. She realised she had been foolish.

'I filled your flask while the water was boiled,' said the kindly Pete. 'I couldn't bear to think of you going all day without a drink.'

'And I saved you some toast,' said Aileen. 'It's gone soggy, but it's better than nothing.'

Tara felt inadequate. She wished neither of them had been so kind. It put her in a difficult position. She felt like the geriatric on the trip...the geriatric or the small child...the one who needed constant help.

On seeing her Joe had crinkled his eyes with a private smile. His mouth had moved slightly at the corners. She answered with a lowering of lashes and a rueful sigh. But the world had changed. The cosy magic of last night had died along with the fire. Low, white clouds interrupted the sun which had only just shown itself over the furthest peak.

When they reached the river—Joe called it a stream but to Tara it was a raging torrent—they were expected to cross it balanced precariously on the wobbly pole. Tara saw it and didn't concern herself. No-one would be able to do that. Surely they'd have to give up and go round. It was only a matter of walking a little further up the valley and using the narrow part which was conveniently dammed with boulders. That, obviously, is what would happen.

So she sat and rested on the bank while Joe, his arms outstretched like a balancing glider, carefully put one foot in front of the other and crossed. He threw his pack down on the far side and waded back into the rushing water, calling to Jeremy to follow him.

'If the water's shallow enough to stand in why can't we just paddle through it?' Tara asked a nervous Pete.

'I think the whole point is that we've got to be brave and attempt to cross the hard way,' he said. Wonder touched his voice as he watched Jeremy flit over the hazard like a ballet-dancer.

'That's ridiculous,' Tara scoffed. 'There's

no way I'm going to do that.'

'No.' Pete was less certain. 'Perhaps it's not so bad when you're actually doing it.'

Tara didn't answer. One by one the others crossed the bridge, aided on both sides by Joe and Jeremy who had positioned themselves at either side in the water. But there was a point, Tara observed, when you had no help from anybody, when if you fell you were hell-bent for a watery destination, a twisted ankle, and worst of all an amusing public display of ineptitude.

Pete went. Pete, scared to death, wobbled all the way across. The look on his face when he arrived and looked back at her made her want to cry. But he quickly sided with the enemy against her and called over, 'Come on, Tara. If I can do it so can you! It's not too bad, I swear!'

Alone on the bank with her rucksack, she approached the pole with trepidation. She stepped on the pole and felt it move.

'Come on, Tara; come on, you can do it!' Joe was watching her, willing her to trust him. His hand was only yards away. Three good steps and she would reach him.

She felt her knees go weak with anger.

How dare he put her in this position! She was helpless...being made a spectacle of in front of everyone else! How dare he? For seconds, while she wobbled there, she hated him. She wanted to reach out and slap his face.

'I can't and I won't,' she said, stepping back, feeling her face rush with blood and her eyes close up with embarrassment. She could feel everybody watching her. She looked up angrily, searching for the slightest sign of laughter. There wasn't any. Everyone was staring, but there was no laughter in their faces. just concern. 'I'm going to take off my boots and wade across,' she told them in a loud, positive voice.

'You'll get your jeans wet.' Joe spoke quietly so only she could hear. 'I'm wearing waterproofs, you're not.'

'I'll roll them up,' she said, with venom in her voice.

'Tara, this water will come up well above your knees. And the current is very strong.'

'I don't care!' Why was she being pushed into this childish position again?

'You'd be better to take off your jeans and come across in your shorts.'

'I haven't got them on, have I?' The sarcasm was lost in the sound of rushing water. 'What shall I do, Joe? Come across in pants?'

'If you like.'

She bit her lip hard and fumed with fury against him...against them all. With her boots tied together high above her head as she'd seen people do in films, she waded into the water. She almost cried out with the cold. It burnt. But she kept all expression from her face as she pushed through the torrent towards him, frightened when she felt the force tearing at her legs, threatening to unbalance her on the slippery rocks she stepped on.

He grabbed her arm and she moaned with relief, but she burned with a blinding anger. She clung to him as her confidence grew, and together they splashed to the bank.

As soon as she was safe she pushed him away with such vehemence that his eyes opened wide.

'Satisfied?' she spat, making sure no-one else could hear.

'Are you?' he replied coolly. 'That's the real question.'

'You mean you think I failed?'

58

'Not at all,' he said. 'You crossed the stream and that's all that matters. It doesn't matter to anyone else how you did it.'

'But it ought to matter to me? Is that what you're saying? I ought to be really upset and feel a failure because I didn't have the courage to cross on that bloody branch?'

He smiled as he shook his head and that made her furious. 'You've got it so wrong,' he said. 'It doesn't matter...OK?'

It was definitely not OK, but people were staring and Jeremy and Simon were moving off and she had to dry her feet and get her boots on and what did she care anyway?

'Are you all right?' Even Pete annoyed her, standing there watching her struggles.

'Yes, I'm all right. I'm just no good at this sort of thing.'

'Well nor am I.'

'But you did it,' she said with bitterness. 'I didn't.'

Pete had the sense to say nothing, and in silence they walked along together.

'Let's hope there aren't too many obstacles of that kind between us and home,' he said eventually.

Tara agreed, and they were friends again. She was glad. She needed a friend, even a traitorous one would do!

'We're going to tie ourselves together with ropes to get down this incline,' Joe was saying, 'just to be on the safe side. The shale is slippery, and if you make a wrong footing you can slide right down.'

It didn't look too steep. A fairly gentle incline down the side of a hill that led to a green valley. But it was a long slope. When they reached the bottom they were going to stop and eat. When they reached the bottom, Joe told them, they were only an hour from home.

An hour from home and two days over, Tara said to herself. Only five days to go and then I can forget any of this ever happened. Life can go back to normal...mum's wedding...get the flat decorated...work as usual. The thought warmed her. Nothing could be as bad as all this walking...it was never-ending.

She still wasn't talking to Joe. She knew she was being childish, but that was the way she felt. She couldn't forgive him for showing her up like that back at the river.

He'd made several attempts to be pleasant. She had rejected them all, stalking along in silence, thinking her bitter thoughts.

'Are you going to be all right doing this?' It was Emma who asked, Emma who had been sticking close to Joe all day like a dog to its master. Tara had heard their laughter come back to her. It had slapped her in the face, an extra sting in the wind, as she'd trudged moodily along.

'It doesn't look too bad. I've just got this thing about water,' she lied, trying to make her smile as genuine as Emma's was.

'Everyone's got something they're afraid of,' Emma confided, her big eyes wide as she crossed her arms protectively. 'I can't stand heights. I go dizzy, and I get this urge to throw myself off to get it over with.'

Is she saying this to make me feel better, Tara asked herself. Or does she mean it? Tara stared at Emma. She was small and compact like a Russian gymnast. She wore her hair tied back from her head in a swinging pony-tail. Suddenly she looked very young, very vulnerable. Her fear showed in her slanting doe-eyes. Confused, Tara said, 'I'm all right with heights. It's just water with me.' How could she admit she feared heights as well? They'd find out soon enough. How could she admit she was frightened of everything, everything that made demands on her physically? But she said to Emma, 'Stick close to me, and you'll be all right,' and could have bitten her tongue out the moment she'd spoken.

Because from the top of the ridge the slope didn't look gentle at all. From the top it looked sheer. But it's not, Tara told herself. It's not from the other angle.

Simon went first of course, while Joe watched over him from the top. Tara held her breath when his head disappeared over the edge, and didn't breathe again until she saw him where the ground levelled out. From there on it looked easy. So it was only the first bit. She'd stopped thinking in terms of herself. She was thinking, now, of Emma.

The rope was clipped to a belt on Tara's waist, and Emma opted to follow her. 'I'll wait for you on that next flat part,' Tara said. 'Just don't panic, that's all. You can't go anywhere. The rope will hold you if you slip.'

Joe looked at her strangely but said

nothing. He patted her arm as she started off, and the same familiar fire tore through her body. She was careful not to look into his eyes. He would know she was afraid. She couldn't fool him, no matter how hard she tried.

All Tara saw as she lowered herself over the rim was the strain on Emma's white face as she stared down into the ghastly space after her. She nervously traversed the flinty shingle, keen to arrive at the flat bit so she could watch for Emma. Before she knew it she was there, and she called back, 'Think about something else, Emma.' Tara was pleased with her new-found ploy. It worked. She had used it. She had thought of Joe. She had thought about last night...his soft words and his soft caresses.

'Talk to me about something then,' Emma's reedy reply came echoing round the corner over the top of the sliding scree. And Tara started to tell her all about Harry French and her mother, and argue as to whether it was sensible they marry or not. When Emma arrived they continued the conversation, with Emma giving her opinions as if she knew the characters as well as Tara did. There was a sudden closeness between the two nervous climbers. It came, like a shaft of lightning, born from the heat of their fear. For a short while it was as if both of them had completely forgotten where they were, and from then it was, as Joe had said, easy going.

'You're shaking,' Emma said when they reached the bottom, hardly able to speak herself through her chattering teeth.

'Am I?' Tara held out her arm and she was. Nothing she could do would make that arm stop trembling. It was like a dithering, jellied extension of herself with a mind of its own. She put it behind her back and held it there with her other hand. 'It's just that I'm tired,' she said. 'I didn't sleep well last night and with all this unfamiliar exertion...'

'You were scared!' Emma looked incredulous. 'You were scared out of your wits and yet you helped me...'

'I wasn't scared.' Tara was determined to carry on the façade although her rubbery legs were making it hard for her to stay upright. 'I've told you, I'm tired. I'm not scared of heights...never have been.'

Then they were watching the others coming down. Tara's heart went out to

Pete. He was certainly a trier! And he didn't mind people knowing how frightened he was. He wasn't ashamed of his fear, not like she was.

'You were brilliant.' Joe had his arm round Emma who leaned her head against his chest, enjoying the close embrace. 'You were terrified and yet you did it!'

'Never again, Joe,' said the girl, simpering and widening her eyes. Is she simpering? Or am I being unkind, Tara wondered. Whatever, she didn't like it, and joined the nerveless Aileen who was finishing her sandwiches, impervious to the drama.

'Home' was in sight when Joe came to walk beside her. 'How are you feeling?' he asked.

'Fine!' She continued walking, her eyes riveted on the little group of distant pines which meant they could stop at last.

'You're a lot fitter than you think...'

She stopped, whirled round and faced him. 'Listen!' she said, her voice shaking in a way she couldn't control. 'I don't want any praise from you. I'm up to here with it all,' she pointed to somewhere vaguely head-high. 'I wish you'd understand that I'm doing this under duress and I don't give a damn whether I'm fit or unfit, whether I succeed or whether I don't. The sooner you get that into your head the happier I will be!'

'Hey! Calm down! You're like a wildcat all of a sudden.' He held her arm and she looked down at his hand, wondering whether to shake it off or not. His eyes caught hers as they came up again, and there was a force behind them that made her catch her breath. Suddenly, she started to laugh. She was nearly home and she could breathe easy again. The tension left her and she was merely Tara Conway, aged twenty-eight, standing on the grass next to the most attractive man she had ever met in her life. She didn't need to prove anything any more. There was no need for this. She liked him. She was attracted to him. And he was no threat to her, was he?

In a quiet voice that made her heart flutter he said, 'That's better! What's it all about anyway? So you don't like exercise... Fine! There are other ways to communicate, you know. I thought we'd found quite a good way last night.'

He squeezed her hand, gave one of his smiles and she melted completely.

'I'll see you later,' he said, and she

watched him walk ahead, the tail of his red checked lumberjack shirt dangling below his windcheater, his pack bouncing on his back. She smiled happily and followed on, bathed in a delightful warmth she couldn't remember feeling before.

But could she handle him? Was he too forceful for someone determined to treat this as an emotional game? She was too happy to worry. She dismissed her fears. She was home and Joe was waiting and no-one had laughed at her today!

Five

Canteen food—greasy, horrible. Normally Tara was careful about what she ate, now she didn't notice. She was watching Joe. He wasn't a vegetarian, not that it mattered.

The teams had gravitated to their own tables. Close as families after a day and a night's experience, there was a security in the company of their associates that didn't extend to outsiders. And it was nice to belong...

She could have chosen salad but her thoughts were elsewhere.

'What makes them do it?' she thought aloud.

'Sorry?' Aileen, next to her, stopped with her fork inches from her mouth. 'What makes who do what?'

'This job.' Tara picked at her food until she saw Aileen looking agitated. Then she took a sensible mouthful. She hadn't always been like this about food. She'd been a glutton, once. And because she was fat they'd thought she was stupid, too. They hadn't believed she had feelings like everybody else. But they never managed to tag that label on her. She came top in everything...except sport.

'Joe Cornel. Doesn't that name ring a bell with you?' Aileen wasn't fat, in spite of what she ate. She was just well-built and it looked right for her. In fact, Tara thought, the more you got to know Aileen the more likeable she was. The loudness was just a front, and Tara knew all about fronts. Underneath all that hearty bonhomie Aileen was intelligent and kind.

Now Tara thought hard. 'No. The name means nothing to me.'

'Joe Cornel Sports...you must know. You see them in every town centre along with the shoe shops and the food chains. It doesn't matter which town you go to these days, the centres all look exactly the same with their paved precincts and their covered walks...'

Tara never took much notice of sports shops, but she recognised the name now. 'Is that him?'

Aileen nodded and continued to shovel in bits of tomato-sauce-covered beefburger.

'Yes. He's not just a pretty face. And he leads one of the most respected mountain rescue teams in the area. But I don't know the answer to your question. I don't know why he does this job. Perhaps he likes it. Perhaps he finds it fulfilling!'

Emma leaned forward. 'Has he told you. about Friday yet?'

'Friday's the last day. I don't care what happens on Friday. It's the one day here I know I'm going to enjoy.'

'They invite the public in!'

'What for?' Again, Tara was abstractedly watching Joe.

'We're given a problem to solve. Something about getting the team to safety. And we have to work it out and put it into practice using the equipment provided. It says something about it at the back of the brochure. And they video it. I think I'm going to go sick on Friday.'

'I'll keep you company.' Tara was all ears. 'I'm not taking part in anything like that.'

It couldn't be true. Emma was the sort of topsy-turvy person who might easily pick up the wrong end of the stick. Tara's stomach turned over at the very thought of having to perform, at her age, in public. She couldn't imagine anything more dreadful. She didn't believe it. Why would the centre invite the public in? It didn't make any sense.

'Then you'll fail the course,' said Aileen. 'Everything else you've done will be null and void. It won't look good on your report. I don't know what your employer's like, but mine wouldn't like it. All that money wasted!'

Pete groaned as he stacked the plates on the table. 'Is there no end to this misery?'

'I'm not going to think about it,' said Tara. 'Maybe it won't really happen.'

After supper they gathered in the hall for a lecture on rock-climbing. Joe wasn't there so Tara nodded off during the slides. She was exhausted. They all believed they should have been given the night off after the last hectic couple of days. And the chairs they sat on were hard. It was exactly like sitting in the school hall.

Puppy-fat, her mother had called it, and there was something sweet and nice in that expression that belied the truth. That was not the description of her condition Tara would have used. Nor would Miss Coles.

Every night, after prep, Miss Coles came

71

to find her no matter where she was hiding. 'Come along, Tara. It's not good you hiding away like this. We've got a lot of work to do before Saturday. You want to impress your mother, don't you?'

'My mother won't be coming, Miss Coles,' Tara would whine, dragging along behind the straight-backed mistress. 'And I don't want to impress anybody. I just want to be left alone.'

'And you don't want to stay fat and unattractive like this for ever, do you?' Miss Coles would go on, looking down at Tara critically.

'I don't care. I honestly don't care.'

'Well you should care! It's unhealthy. It's unpleasant.'

Stripped to her vest and knickers, Tara would make an embarrassed entrance into the gym where those girls who were keen were working out.

Every piece of equipment was to be used for the demonstration. Every rope, every wall-bar, every box and every horse. And to take part Tara had to be able to use them all. The whole performance was to be done to music. Miss Coles chose the *Sugar Plum Fairy*, and that music blasted out with terrible distortion, thudding out

72

a frighteningly fast time as Tara took her place for the practice run.

She wasn't as fat as she imagined she was. She certainly wasn't disgusting. But in her own mind, the eyes of the audience would glue themselves to her just because she looked so awful. If only they were allowed to wear short skirts. If only they were allowed to wear blouses.

She was the only one doing the display who couldn't climb a rope. In the end Miss Coles said that in order not to disrupt the display she could just sit on the knot at the bottom and swing. She managed to climb the wall-bars and hang there upside down. But her heart sank when she imagined what she must look like...all that fat flopping down.

She could do somersaults on the mats. She could do handstands against the wall. What she feared most was vaulting the horse, and doing a move called 'waterfall' on the box. She had to leap up on it, do a handstand on the end and let herself go right over onto the floor.

'Come on, Tara! You can do it!'

I know I can do it, Miss Coles, she would have liked to have shrieked. It's just that I hate doing it. It makes me so frightened! And I can't see what point there is in being frightened.

When the big day came the parents would be sitting on a raised stage at one end of the enormous room. It would accommodate a hundred. All the staff would be there. The gym display was one of many such events taking place during parents' weekend. Tara would have liked to be in the play, but she'd gone for an audition and not been chosen. 'Your acting is good, Tara, but there's no part for a large person in this play. Wait until we do *Midsummer Night's Dream* next year. I promise you a part as one of the rude mechanicals, or maybe even Bottom the weaver.'

She was poked into wakefulness by Pete. 'Come and have some coffee,' he said. Her heart was beating nineteen to the dozen, and she wiped her sweating hands. 'Bad dreams?' he asked.

Tara nodded. 'I must be more tired than I think,' she said. 'Dropping off like that in the middle of the lecture. It's lucky I didn't fall off my chair!'

When she saw Joe chatting to a group at the far end of the recreation room she felt her temperature soar. In a red woollen sweater with a white collar sticking up underneath, he looked dark, sensual and amazing. He sat there as if he didn't know it, one leg crossed over the other, while admirers sat round listening, hanging onto his every word.

She knew he had seen her. He gave no sign but she knew.

Well, if he could sit with a group of admirers around him, so could she.

In the end she hadn't done anything to lose weight. It had just happened. And with the weight had gone the unkindness she had had to endure for so long. People were suddenly nice to her, their attitudes were different. She looked a world away from the chubby, shy little girl with the pigtails. She let her hair down and chose her clothes with care. Her complexion was flawless throughout her teenage years, as if to compensate for the earlier horror. She was sought after, she was wildly attractive, and she had developed a brilliant acting style. But it was far from real... She knew what people were like—underneath.

Now she threw herself into her role with energy. She wasn't going to mope and wait around for Joe Cornel to shed his groupies and come over. Let him see she wasn't so unpopular herself...

She sat so she could see him out of the corner of her eye but carefully didn't look in his direction. She chose a lively group, and Pete was the obvious choice for her attentions. She would start with Pete, she decided, and then the others would vie for her charms. This was the part she played at work. The customers liked it. Everyone liked it...except her.

It worked, as it always did. She started by asking personal questions, people always liked that. Then she listened, with special interest. Then she brought her wit to play...she could be very funny and vivacious when she wanted to be. At this stage they were hers.

Satisfactory, loud laughter was coming from their table. She took a chance and looked across the room at Joe. Damn it! Their eyes met. She looked away and tried to make it seem she was scanning the room for someone else but it was too late! She hoped he didn't realise this was all for his benefit.

Time went by quickly. She glanced at her watch. It was late. She was afraid Pete was taking her flirtatious manner too seriously. It was time to back off. Where was Joe? She looked across the room again. He was gone!

'I'm tired,' she said flatly. 'I'm going to bed.'

'Stay for a bit longer. I was just beginning to enjoy myself.'

The expressions on the faces of her new-found friends all agreed with Pete. Couldn't they see she was using them? Couldn't they see this wasn't the real Tara Conway at all? They wouldn't have liked the real one. They had seen her briefly this morning, by the river below Craig-fawr. Frightened, cowardly, slim on the surface but fat and flabby underneath...

It was dark. The arc of light from the moth-blown bulb outside the recreation room soon ran out, so did the sound of voices. Tara set off in the direction of chalet seven, stepping carefully on the uneven ground. There were night sounds here that were different from those in the city.

She leapt back, clutching her heart, when she recognised him. He was waiting for her, leaning back against a chalet wall with his arms crossed.

'Are you avoiding me?' he asked, not moving. 'I'd saved a place for you. You went and sat at the other end of the room.'

Tara felt silly. 'I expected you to come over,' she said, still shocked at the unexpectedness of the meeting.

'I'm on duty,' he told her. 'I can't just leave the clients in order to be alone with you, much as I'd like to.'

This made sense. Why hadn't she realised? Why had she assumed he was playing games with her? They were both too old for that sort of nonsense. She wasn't sure, but she would have put him in his early thirties, and she, at twenty-eight, was old enough to know better.

'Let's walk,' he said, pushing himself off the wall and laying his arm across her shoulder. 'You're still a mystery. I want to know you.'

The murmur she'd heard in the background turned out to be a river that splashed down from the rocks in a waterfall and meandered through the pines. They sat on a boulder beside a pool and watched the moonlight turn the water silver.

'Why were you avoiding me?' He wouldn't leave it alone. 'Why did you ignore me tonight? Anyone would think we were strangers.'

'I felt it would be rude to leave my group.' She always lied well. She never lacked a quick answer.

'I see.' He wasn't satisfied but it would do. He turned to stare at her and she looked away, feeling his eyes over her body and trembling as if he were touching her with his hands. 'I'm surprised you are alone,' he said softly. 'Someone who looks like you.'

People always judged you on the outside, they never looked within. That's what made it easy.

'I nearly wasn't,' she said. 'I was engaged until last year.'

'Oh?' He wasn't going to ask. He waited to see if she wanted to tell him.

'His name was Mathew. We were together for four years.'

'That's a long time.'

'It wasn't any good.' She clasped her knees and took a deep breath of pine-filled air. 'It was doomed from the start.'

'Why?'

'He wanted too much of me,' she said. 'He didn't approve of my independence.' She always said that. It sounded good and was vague enough for people not to know what she meant.

79

'What do you mean?'

Tara was startled. This was the first time anyone had questioned her. Her head, dizzy from his nearness, found it hard to assemble reasonable explanations. For once in her life she was stumped.

'I don't like to talk about it.' she said weakly.

'I want to know,' he insisted, taking her hand and stroking it.

'And he didn't like me as I was. He wanted to change me.'

'I find that hard to believe.' He talked softly for someone who posed such a threat.

How could she tell Joe Cornel about her fear of sex? How could she speak of the terror she felt over her nakedness...not just physical nakedness but the nakedness and honesty required for love? It was her fault, not Mathew's. He had been patient, he had waited for long enough. Finally he had given up, and in his pain he had called her such names...he had hated her, yes he had, at the end. And he'd been right. She was a frigid bitch! She was a selfish whore! But those were things you couldn't talk about sitting by a moonlit pool under whispering trees with a man who set your heart on fire.

80

Shadows...would she always be surrounded by these terrible shadows? Tara shivered and he kissed her, long, passionately and sensually. She responded with an eagerness that astonished her. She wanted more! She wanted to get closer! But she was afraid.

'And you?' she asked at last. 'You're not involved with anyone else?'

He was quiet for a while before he answered, 'I've been too busy proving myself.' His smile was sad. 'I built up an empire, I climbed every mountain I could find. It seems I was going in the wrong direction all the time, doesn't it? I didn't leave myself room for personal relationships. And sometimes they're the hardest challenges of all, aren't they?'

They held each other as they had done up by the lake. Every sensation was multiplied a thousand times. Tara felt like sobbing under the power of her feelings. She was overwhelmed by them. She'd never met anyone like Joe Cornel before, or if she had, she had blocked them out. She couldn't block him out and she didn't want to. But she was very frightened. She didn't want to see, no matter how far away in the future it was, the hatred in his face she'd seen in Mathew's. She didn't want to hear those words on his lips or watch him walk away, turning his back on her forever. And she knew she would. If she continued with this, she would...

It seemed she could go so far and no further.

Six

'How would it be if I chucked this in and came back to work? How would Paul feel about that?'

Wanda was the person to ask. As Paul's personal secretary, she knew him better than anyone. Tara had picked her time carefully. She was telephoning at half past nine in the morning. Paul was never normally in before ten.

'Chuck it in? Is it as bad as that?'

Tara imagined how the smile would be spreading over Wanda's face and clutched the receiver tightly. Wanda knew damn well how bad it was likely to be. It was hard to speak without being overheard as it was. She was standing in the open foyer of the reception hut. They'd made an effort and put coarse matting down. Foyer was too grand a word, but that's what she supposed it would be called.

'It's not just the course, although that's as horrific as I knew it would be. It's this man...'

'Don't tell me you've gone and got yourself involved again.'

'This is serious, Wanda. I need to leave here. I need to leave NOW, before it's too late. Paul wouldn't really mind, would he? Did he really expect me to stick it out?'

She heard the horn of the mini-bus honk outside. They were waiting for her. She was holding up the whole group.

Wanda knew all about Mathew. And she was the only person who'd been told the real reasons for the break-up. Tara had discussed her problems over and over and over again with her closest friend. Their sessions had gone on late into the night. They never managed to come to any conclusions. Perhaps it was the wine they tended to drink when they were together that confused the issue. Wanda kept suggesting that Tara would feel differently with the right man, but Tara wasn't convinced. Anyway, she considered Wanda wasn't being too helpful now.

'He thinks this experience is going to loosen you up a bit, Tara, and who knows, he might be right. You know how important he considers these newfangled training methods. You don't need me to tell you that. He's got a bee in his bonnet at the moment. It'll pass.'

'But how would he feel if I called it a day?'

'You know Paul. He hates quitters. He'd think you were being unreasonable. Making a drama out of a crisis...all that stuff...'

'So you wouldn't advise it?'

'I wouldn't advise it at all. I think you've got to stick it out, whatever happens. By the way...what's he like?'

Wanda could be extremely irritating at times. 'I've got to go. They're waiting for me in the mini-bus. We're going rock-climbing.'

Wanda groaned. 'Oh, you poor thing. I'm just having my first coffee of the morning. I'll dunk a biscuit for you...'

The money ran out and Tara pulled a face into the speaker. So much for friendship, she said to herself as she picked up her pack and pushed through the swing doors.

They went, like children, huddled in the back of a van that wound and ground its way sickeningly along the twisting roads. Just like children, thought Tara, trying to ignore the effect Joe's eyes were having on her through the driving-mirror. She had decided what she was going to do. She was going to fake an accident. That would either allow her to go home, which would solve everything, or get her out of future activities for the rest of the week. Plots and plans scuttled through her mind like leggy black spiders. From her point of view she had little alternative.

And as for Joe...she didn't have a scheme for him. But she'd think of one. Somehow she'd pull out before the damage was done.

Pete was all over her this morning. She had gone too far last night...been too nice. Now she was in danger of hurting him. She closed her eyes. She couldn't bear it. He looked as if he was always hurt. Why was life so cruel?

Out of the van and they clanked off up the hill, carrying the climbing gear. One look at the tall crag was enough for Tara. Joe could say, 'This is nothing' as much as he liked. He might influence the others...not her. It was like a fang in a dog's lower jaw, and just as smooth and sharp. There was hardly room at the top to sit, let alone collapse as she would need to. No. Now was the time to take action.

She yelped with pain and sat down.

She squeezed her eyes up and the tears obediently came. Her face crumpled, and she rocked backwards and forwards as though in great anguish.

Pete, all concern, was immediately at her side. She'd known he would be. 'What is it? What have you done?'

'It's nothing...it'll pass. I've gone over on my ankle. It happens, sometimes. I should have worn my support bandage.'

He delved in his rucksack and brought out a ragged tissue. 'Dry your eyes,' he said, 'and let me get your boot off. There'll be some nasty swelling if we're not careful.'

He tried to ease it off and she shouted, 'Oh God no! Leave it alone! Don't touch it!'

'You have hurt yourself,' he said, his face full of sympathy. He ran helpless hands through tousled, sandy hair. He looked accusingly at the ground. 'Where did it happen...?'

'I don't know. I think I must have stepped in a hollow. I felt it go.'

Everyone gathered round her. 'She's twisted her ankle.' Pete took control. 'She's in agony. She can't bear it touched.'

They made a space for Joe. He did

not look at her ankle. He watched her face and she saw his expression harden. 'That's unfortunate,' he said. 'Considering what we were about to do. It looks as if you'll have to spectate for the rest of the day, doesn't it?'

'I can't put any weight on it,' she said, pathetically trying.

'No. I don't expect you can,' he said. 'It's surprising how sharp these sprains can be. And isn't it funny how they always happen when you least expect them?'

He didn't believe her, but he wasn't prepared to show her up in front of the rest of the group. For that she supposed she must be grateful. She knew he despised her for what she was doing, but what alternative was there? Saying she wasn't going to do it wouldn't have worked. It wasn't as if it was a matter of life or death! If Tara Conway never climbed a rock in her life the world wouldn't suffer for it.

She sat in a knoll at the bottom of the rock in the sunshine and enjoyed herself. She wished she'd brought a book. When she saw the others climbing, she knew she'd done the right thing. Nothing on earth would induce her to do that!

But she was concerned for Emma. The girl's face was ashen as she waited for her turn.

'Emma,' she whispered, calling her over. 'Pretend to be ill! There's nothing wrong with me and I've managed to get out of it. You could have eaten something that disagreed with you. Easy, when you think about last night's meal.'

'I can't act as well as you can,' Emma said. 'They'd see right through me!'

'Well just refuse!' Tara encouraged. It was easy to be brave for somebody else. 'Say you won't do it. Go on! I'll stand up for you!'

Emma shook her head. 'I want to be able to do it,' she said. 'I know I'll feel such a sense of achievement if I manage.'

Tara was baffled. She had no such thoughts, and couldn't understand anyone who had.

'But I would be grateful if you would talk to me,' she told Tara. 'Like you did coming down the hill. Just a few encouraging words...you know.'

It was the least Tara could do. And she was half demented with worry by the time Emma's turn came up. Watching Pete had been bad enough. The sweat had poured off Tara as she had watched him go, stuck to the rock face like a limpet, every move a hair-raising effort. Tara had fallen back, exhausted, when his boots finally disappeared over the top where Joe waited. Pete had waved triumphantly down at her. She was pleased for him. She felt he needed a few successes.

Now Joe, full of enthusiasm, shouted down to Emma. Jeremy, at the bottom, gave sensible words of advice.

'Fingers crossed,' Emma called to Tara, red ribbon disappearing under the helmet. Tara felt more and more fraudulent, and crossed her fingers tightly to make up for it.

'God, I can't watch,' she said to herself as she heard the first scramblings of her friend. This was almost worse than doing it...but not quite!

Emma was stuck. She was halfway up and unable to go on. 'I just can't move,' she shouted up to Joe. 'I seem to have lost all feeling in my legs.'

'Don't worry about it.' Joe sounded easy. Tara knew he was not. 'Just rest. just wait. You'll be all right in a minute. It's nerves.'

Minutes came and went with the speed of years. Fluffy clouds danced by overheard, immune to the drama. Summer could have given way to autumn for all Tara knew. And Emma was still stuck. Jenny screamed at her from the top. 'Don't let go, Emma...just don't let go. Someone'll come and get you...hang on!'

Emma was sobbing now. Tara could hear her. The sound echoed back off the awful rock face. She could stay still no longer. She couldn't stand it! She got up with no sign of a limp, raced to the foot of the cliff and called up, 'I'm here, right underneath you. Nothing's going to happen to you, Emma. You're hardly off the ground. Even I wouldn't be frightened to be where you are. Jeremy's coming up to lift you down.'

'Talk to me. Just keep talking to me...' The desperate fear in Emma's voice struck such deep chords in Tara.

'That's what I'm doing...'

'I should have done what you did, pretended I was hurt.'

'I'll give you some lessons in real cowardice before we come out again.'

'Promise?'

'I promise. I'm expert at it.'

And all the time, at a snail-slow pace, Jeremy was making his way up the crag towards the terrified girl.

'Tell me more about Harry French.'

'Harry French is not good enough for my mother, as I was telling you yesterday. The only good thing about him is that he makes her laugh. I ask you, is that a good enough basis for marriage?'

'I'd marry someone who could make me laugh just now.'

'They've been friends for years. Lovers, I suppose. Though I don't like to think about my mother having a lover.'

'Does he like you?'

'Does Harry French like me? It's something I haven't thought about much. But no, I don't think he does.' Tara tried to keep the hysteria from her voice, tried to keep the tone conversational. 'I think he knows I am against the marriage. He probably thinks I stick my nose in where it's not wanted. He'd be happier if I was married myself and out of his hair, I think. He doesn't want to take a spinster daughter on board. Emma, Jeremy's coming over from your right-hand side. You'll feel him next to you in a minute. He's going to put a safety sling around you and lower you down to the ground. Do you understand? You don't have to move. You just wait where you are and let it happen. OK?'

'OK.'

'And I'm pouring a cup of tea down here ready for when you arrive. Do you take one or two sugars?'

'I don't take sugar. But I don't think I'll care whether it's sweet or not by the time I get down there.'

'Got you!' Jeremy lowered the frightened girl to the ground...a wretched bundle of laundry. Tara spoke soothingly from below, afraid that at the last minute Emma might panic and put Jeremy himself in danger.

At last she could wrap her arms round Emma. 'My God, Emma, you gave me the fright of my life,' she said, ridiculously near to tears.

Emma was crying. She seemed overly upset about Tara's lie. 'You've given yourself away,' she said.

'What do you mean?'

'Your ankle! They'll know you haven't twisted it now. And it's my fault.'

'Emma, I couldn't give a damn about

that!' It seemed so unimportant after the drama of the last ten minutes. 'That's the last thing on my mind.'

'Joe won't be too pleased.'

'Well Joe can take a running jump.'

'You keep pretending you don't care. Everyone knows you do. Everyone's seen you together...'

'I'd rather stay alive than climb to please Joe Cornel.' Tara wrapped Emma in a blanket, and watched and fussed over her as she sipped the hot tea.

'I don't know what came over me,' Emma said over and over again. 'I went rigid. It was like being paralysed.'

Tara nodded. She knew the feeling of old.

'At least I wasn't the only one who didn't do it,' she said to Tara. 'At least I'm not the only failure!'

'At least you tried.' Tara, however, believed it was better not to.

'One thing's for certain. I'll never forget it. I don't know what I'd have done if you hadn't been there.'

'Nothing could have happened to you. Think about it. You were attached to the rock by ropes!'

'It certainly didn't feel that way from up

94

there.' Emma looked up at the fatal spot and shivered. She clutched her blanket around her.

Emma was the star of the show. She was quickly surrounded by sympathisers who, one by one, scaled down the rock face. Each one of them, apart from Joe and perhaps Simon and Jeremy, was surprised the same thing hadn't happened to them. They understood. They knew how she felt. If there had been an award Emma would have been given it.

Tara had completely forgotten about Pete. He came and stood quietly beside her. 'Your ankle, it isn't so bad then?'

Tara blushed. There was nothing for it. She had to tell him the truth. 'It was a ruse to get out of climbing,' she said, hoping he would laugh.

'Why didn't you tell me that?' he said. 'There was no need to fool me, too. I am on your side, you know.'

'I'm sorry, Pete, I didn't think.' What else could she say?

'I was really worried about you. I nearly didn't climb myself, so I could stay with you.'

'There was no need for that. I am quite capable of looking after myself. I've done it for years, and I expect I'll manage to carry on doing it.'

He looked as if she had slapped him on the face. Pete had been a hero today. Of all the climbers, excluding Emma, he had been the most nervous. And yet, with little fuss, he had scaled the rock. At the very back of her mind she knew he had done it to impress her. Now, because of Tara, he was miserable and dejected, his big day was ruined. It was all her fault...all to do with her silly behaviour. Yes, she could have confided in him. But she'd needed him to reinforce her story. She just hadn't thought.

She couldn't dismiss him as a weak-minded fool because it was she who had egged him on last night in order to play out her little scenario in front of Joe. But she hadn't meant to hurt him. She hadn't expected Emma to need her like that.

'Satisfied with your performance today?' Joe's voice was full of scorn. The expression on his face was chiselled firm...his mouth a tight straight line. He loomed very large with his ropes over his shoulder. She leapt to her own defence.

'Don't start blaming me because something went wrong on your precious

96

expedition! It wasn't my fault Emma got stuck!'

'I'm not talking about Emma. I'm talking about decent, innocent people getting hurt.'

'I thought that was my business.' She knew her eyes were sparking. And through it all she felt sick inside.

'It's my business when we need to be a close-knit group. When trusting each other can make the difference between life and death!' There were flecks of amber in his freezing eyes, crystals bedded in blue ice. 'Nothing matters but Tara Conway, does it? Poor little badly-done-to Tara.'

'How dare you...'

'That's the one thing I'm good at... daring. Ask anybody. I dare to do anything. But I'm beginning to wonder if I dare trust you, when other people's feelings can mean so little...'

He walked away. She followed on behind, her heart bleeding under the pain of his attack. Tara knew all about unkindness. And yet the times she had used it herself, unknowingly, for protection... She didn't see herself as an unkind person. She certainly didn't mean to be. She hadn't realised that Joe was aware of everything that was going on in his group. Maybe he had to be.

She allowed her anger to flood in, along with a manufactured sense of injustice. She wasn't responsible for Pete! If he had read the messages wrong it was his fault and he'd have to learn. She'd wanted to get out of her involvement with Joe and now it had happened she was glad!

She sat at the back in the van, apart from everyone else. This was how she was going to play it from now on. Let Joe Cornel write a stinging report to Gilpins. Tara knew she wouldn't lose her job. It might just take a bit longer to get promoted, that's all.

Her first impressions had been right. She should have stuck to them. He was just the sort of poser she detested!

Seven

She felt that nobody liked her. She felt they all knew how she'd treated Pete and every one of them was disgusted, as Joe undoubtedly was. No wonder Tara withdrew. If she could have done, she would have made herself ugly, because that's how she felt. But that was not possible.

There were discussions on the way the course was going this evening. She would have missed them if she could have been bothered. She would have devised some cunning excuse. As it was she went along, protected by the undaunted Aileen.

With her eyes well down she entered the hall. What good this was doing as far as her career was concerned she couldn't imagine. It would take months for her to get her confidence back, confronted as she was with all this failure.

She couldn't stop her heart lurching when she saw Joe. He sat on the edge of a semicircle of chairs. He looked casual and relaxed...happy even! He didn't care about the rift between them...and nor did she. It took every ounce of courage she had to delve down and find the energy to light herself up. It took everything she'd ever practised to put that mask on, make her mouth smile and put interest in her eyes. But she did it. She even made herself listen to what they were talking about.

'We're halfway through the course,' she heard Joe's voice saying. 'And this is a chance for you to say what you think. I want you to be honest. If there's anything that wants changing we're open to change. If there's anything you want to work on, we'll work on it.'

There was an embarrassing silence. Tara squirmed in her chair. She'd always hated this sort of thing. Normally she made herself say something to ease the tension. She wasn't going to do that tonight! It was someone else's turn.

'Well I'm thoroughly enjoying it.' This was Aileen. Who else? 'I like the closeness that's grown between us. And I like the way we're all made to feel important in everything we do. For me, it's good to learn to depend on other people. I tend to take over situations and feel I'm the only one who can be trusted to finish a job properly...' She tapered off. But the ball was in the court.

Joe was rolling his pen between finger and thumb. As was his habit, one leg crossed the other, and Tara had noticed before how he swung backwards and forwards slightly when he sat in front of an audience.

She was surprised to hear Emma pipe up. 'I've done things I thought were impossible.' She gave an embarrassed giggle, astonished, it sounded, that she was speaking up. 'I know what happened today was terrible, but I know I've gained from it. And I feel better, physically. It's the exercise and the fresh air, I suppose. I think, now, that I could tackle anything, you know...?' She ended with a question, and people nodded politely.

'Well this is all very nice.' Tara felt Joe's eyes on her. She didn't need to look, she just knew they were there. They flickered off her and round the group. 'As I see it, the main purpose of a course like this is to allow people to find things out about themselves that they didn't know before. Good or bad, it doesn't matter. It is a way of discovering ourselves, and the more we

101

understand ourselves, what motivates us, what makes us tick, the stronger we are.'

How glib it all was...and how easy for him to sit there and say it. Joe Cornel, cool, self-assured, who was afraid of nothing and who turned all he touched into gold! Tara winced as she imagined what he must be thinking. This place must be a little goldmine...as if he needed the money with his chain of shops! Wanda had told her how much a place on the course cost. She could be staying at a first-class hotel in the middle of Greece. She wished she was.

'There must be some of you who didn't want to come. Some of you who thought it a waste of time...who still do...?' Joe finished with a question as Emma had, but it was a question nobody was honestly prepared to answer. It seemed to Tara as if he was reading her mind, now, as well as her face. Had the question been aimed deliberately at her?

'I've been surprised at the strength of my concern for the other people in the group, people I hadn't even met three days ago.' Pete deliberately hadn't sat next to Tara. There had been a space there when he arrived. Yesterday he would have taken it.

Tonight he was sitting opposite. Tara felt guiltier than ever.

His voice was firm and sure. He didn't sound like a man who'd been badly done to. 'It makes my own struggles seem small when I see the courage of some of the others.' Some of the others? Was he excluding her? The one person in the group who clearly had no courage? 'Yesterday,' he said, 'I remember watching Tara helping Emma down the hill. She was scared to death, but she didn't show it.' Stop it, Pete. Tara willed him to shut up. I don't need this sort of protection! She was desperately trying to keep a low profile, and in the circumstances Pete's praise of her was the last thing she needed. It made her behaviour towards him seem worse!

Now Joe was leaning forward, resting his chin on his hand. Who did he think he was? A psychiatrist as well as everything else? 'And what about those of you who have done this sort of thing before. Jeremy? Simon? Paul and Clive? Are you getting anything out of this?'

'I don't think they are helpful enough.' Jenny was normally the quiet one, but she spoke up now in her sensible-sounding voice. 'They go on ahead, doing their own thing. They seem to have a private competition of their own going on. If it wasn't for Joe constantly bringing them back, they'd have split the group in two by now.'

'Is that right?' Joe asked a general question. Obviously most people thought it was but didn't like to say so. Joe, Tara noticed, was clever at never giving his own opinion.

'I think it started pretty much that way. I think that's changing each day.' Simon, the accused, sounded concerned. 'It was much more noticeable today how people were working together instead of trying to win.'

'It's hard to offer too much help without offending people,' said Jeremy. 'Some people like to feel they've done it on their own. They resent interference.'

'Has that been your experience?'

'Not here, but in the past, yes.'

'Would anybody here feel they would rather cope alone? Would any of you resent being helped?'

Tara felt a flush starting in her hands and working its way to her face. Her legs were tightly crossed, and she gripped one slippery hand in the other. She wished this was over. It was getting much too personal. She hated being helped! She always had! She'd always felt she ought to be able to cope on her own, and was a failure if she couldn't.

Once again Joe was a success! Did he ever fail at anything? He'd started a lively discussion. Everybody joined in. They all had a point of view and formality flew out of the window. Now, only if you were loud enough could you be heard. Every now and then Joe interrupted to bring them back to the point, but everyone was enjoying themselves immensely. Tara noticed that, otherwise, Joe did not contribute. Nor, of course, did she.

He was staring at her again, wondering why she wasn't joining in, probably. By her behaviour alone she was showing him how hurt she was. Gradually, the truth of this dawned, and she made a deliberate decision to break in somewhere. Whatever else happened, Joe mustn't know the strength of her feelings. But she had left it too late. She hadn't yet spoken. She had been left behind.

'I hate it!'

Nobody heard her. She was sitting back in her chair and her voice was muffled.

They were all leaning forward. So she stood up, miserable beyond endurance. They were missing the point completely! There were people in this world for whom this sort of thing was a nightmare.

'I hate it!' This time they did hear. There was a sudden, awful silence. Tara sat down again, and gripped the seat of her chair. Faces were turned in her direction, faces full of questions.

'Every moment of it is agony,' she said, exaggerating to make her point. 'I can't wait for it to be over so I can go home. Nothing on earth would make me come on this sort of thing ever again.'

She could see them all thinking, wondering how to react to this outburst, wondering who this person was, the opposite of the confident character she had disguised herself as last night. She felt she had to speak again because no-one else was going to. 'You can talk away all you like about the benefits of this sort of thing,' she said, sounding, to her relief, a fraction more reasonable. 'But people aren't all made the same way. Some people can't do it!'

Horror dawned as she felt the prick of tears in her eyes. Don't let me cry, she prayed, oh God don't let me cry. I don't want them to know how badly I feel! 'And it's not fair,' she choked her way along the sentence, 'to make people do things when they are so frightened.'

'I had no idea it was so difficult for you. You gave the impression that you weren't interested, not that you were really, seriously nervous.' Aileen sat back on her chair puffing out her cheeks, her eyes round with surprise. 'You were always laughing, scornful about it all...'

'Pete knew. I told Pete I was frightened because I knew he was as well. But it turned out that he wasn't, not really. He was just pretending. He didn't chicken out of anything. Not like I did.'

When was Joe going to say something? It was his responsibility to turn the conversation round, away from her again. Couldn't he see how awful this was for her? Where was he? They were all staring at her as if she was a madwoman, an alien, or something unpleasant that had crawled out from under the carpet...

She turned to face him. He was to blame for all this! Without his silly course she could be sitting at home in front of the TV, or lost in a decent book. She was ready to shout at him, ready to accuse him of the first thing that came into her mind...attack! Attack! She wanted someone to attack until she saw his face.

It was almost as if he wasn't listening. He was away somewhere in a world of his own, and his eyes had taken on a look of such gentle understanding, a look of such knowing, that she felt, in spite of her fury, his own silent pain stab her heart.

Lost without a victim, Tara whirled round and left the room, tears of frustration blurring her vision. She had left them discomfited, she had broken into the little self-satisfied world they had created around themselves, and she was mortified! She'd have to face them all in the morning. There were three more days of this to go! She had made a complete and utter fool of herself. Her image had shattered, her mask had cracked in half.

She pretended to be asleep when they all came in. She didn't want to talk to anybody. She hadn't worked out what she was going to say, or what part she was going to play.

She wanted Joe to hold her again, to start again with him from the beginning. She knew he had the strength she needed to get herself over this...it was more than just missing that closeness with Joe, it was something about losing herself. And yet it was over, whatever had been between them. Never again would she feel the strength of his arms or the tenderness of his kisses. Never again would his mouth brush past her ear as his soft voice told her things. Surely this was what she'd wanted? Only this morning she had wanted to escape. But now, in her unhappiness, in her loneliness, she wanted Joe.

She got up quietly when the room was silent, slipped on her shoes, pulled a stiff, grey blanket over her nightdress and made her way through the darkness back to the place where they had last been alone together. The water splashing into the pool played the same tune. But her heart did not. Then, just a short while ago, she had been happy. Now she felt the whole weight of her heart as it broke.

She sat just thinking by herself.

'Do you mind if I join you?' For a breath-stopping moment she thought it was Joe. It was Pete. She smiled and tried not to show her disappointment. She had been unkind enough already to this shy man. 'I betrayed you back there,' he said, sitting where Joe had sat last night and scuffing up pine needles with his foot. 'I feel the same way as you, and yet I never said so. Not with the conviction you did. I wanted to say it, I wanted to support you, but I didn't.'

Tara shook her head, surprised. She wasn't sure what he was talking about. 'It doesn't matter, Pete. You don't owe me anything. I understand.'

'I feel bad about it.'

'Don't. You shouldn't always feel so badly about yourself.' She smiled to herself. Was it her saying that?

When his arm went around her, she let herself fall back against it, needing to feel the warmth of a friend. He stroked her hair and she let him, wishing she could be a little girl again...but a different one. In his way, Pete was a very attractive man, tall, with the kind of face they always use on adverts...ordinary and yet with a charm... There was nothing unusual about his face as there was about Joe's.

'I don't think I have ever met anyone quite so beautiful in my whole life.'

His words were unexpected and yet, in the atmosphere, in the darkness, they sounded oddly natural. 'I wish I could spend the rest of my life just sitting here under the pine-trees with you in my arms?'

Oh if only he was Joe! If only it was Joe sitting here next to her, keeping her warm and whispering into the breeze. She closed her eyes and let herself pretend. Joe felt firmer...Joe smelt of wool...and Joe's voice was deeper and he spoke more slowly. And if Joe was here she would not be feeling cold. She would be feeling alive and beautiful, clever and charming...no, Pete was not Joe.

'I've been using you.' Tara had to stop him feeling this way about her. 'I've been using you in order to get my own way...I have a habit of doing that to people.'

'That's what I'm here for,' said Pete. 'I want you to use me. I want to serve you in any way I can.'

'You shouldn't think that way about yourself, Pete,' she said uneasily. 'You put yourself down too much. You deserve better. You're a very loveable, charming man. And a brave one, too. Look at the way you climbed that cliff this afternoon.'

'I did it for you.'

Tara was embarrassed. This was becoming more and more difficult. How could she tell him, without hurting him again, that she wasn't interested in anything but a friendly relationship with him? He was holding her tightly now, but she hadn't the heart to pull away.

'Pete,' she started to say. 'You've got it wrong. I don't want you to do things for me. I like you very much...I'm fond of you, but...' He silenced her with a gentle kiss, so unexpected that she wasn't ready.

'I know better,' he said. She could feel his body trembling beside her.

A movement behind them...almost un-detectable...a change in the breeze, a bending of the pine carpet... Tara would never know what it was that caught her attention. But she knew he was there just seconds before he spoke.

'I'm sorry.' Joe's voice was low and hardly audible over the splashing water. 'I wouldn't have disturbed you.'

Tara whipped round, Pete's arms falling from her shoulders. 'Joe? I was waiting for you, but Pete...' She sounded so terribly insincere! At this, the most urgent moment in her life, her voice, her facial movements, they were all betraying her!

'Don't worry, Tara.' In contrast, Joe was horribly honest. 'I knew you'd be here. I just wanted to make sure you were all right. I see you are. I'll say goodnight.'

'Goodnight!' Pete was the only one of the three with a voice left to speak.

Tara strained to hear the last receding footstep, the last crackling branch. She heard nothing. Only silence. Even the normal night sounds were gone. She sat on the boulder as if she was fixed there in stone, a statue to the nymph of the mountain river, cold, stiff, and unable even to cry.

Eight

After that there was no need to tell Pete anything.

He gave a low groan. 'I've really messed things up for you, haven't I?'

She felt she couldn't stand a display of self-deprecation from Pete. She was surprised when she didn't get it.

'I think I must love him,' said Tara. 'Or why would it hurt so much?'

'I'll make it right,' Pete told her. 'I'll talk to him in the morning...now if you like!'

'It's no good, Pete. It's not just you,' she explained. 'We're really totally unsuited!' And still the tears wouldn't come. 'It's not as if I even know him! We've only just met!'

Completely exposed, with the hurt inside her red raw, she didn't care any more about letting anyone see her torment. She needed help. She couldn't stand the pain.

Pete sat quietly beside her, giving her anxious sideways glances, unable to take it away. But the fact that he was there

114

helped. She needed to talk. Not about Joe...anything rather than Joe. She soon forgot that she had company, and talked, as if to herself, about things she didn't even like to think of. Why, she wondered, did all this come to surface just now? Weren't things bad enough without delving back into the past?

'I've never been able to handle relation-ships,' Tara told him, sounding slurred in her sadness, as if she had been drinking.

'You're not alone in that,' Pete com-miserated. 'Look at the fool I've made of myself in the last couple of days.'

'I'm fond of you, Pete,' she said. 'You're one of the nicest people I've ever met.'

'Stop it, Tara,' he said. 'You're only making me feel worse.'

'It started going wrong for me a long time ago,' she said, thinking hard. 'I think it was when I was quite small. I must have been ten or eleven...'

Her mother hadn't come to the gym display. Everyone but Tara was sorry. She was glad! Her mother was the only one who loved her. She didn't want her mother to see her in this, her worst light.

Tara had begun to believe this dreaded

115

day would never come. Perhaps, in some magic way, it wouldn't, if she wished it enough. On the Saturday morning, when she woke, she felt as if some familiar yet terrible monster was sitting on her bed, squeezing her chest. And then she remembered, and tried to escape back into sleepy oblivion again.

She listed the possibilities in her head. She could run away...but the consequences of that would be too dreadful. And if she did that, she would have to admit to her mother that she hated the school. Then her mother's life, as well as her own, would be ruined.

She could say she was sick. But Miss Coles would be looking out for that. It was a hackneyed, overplayed ploy which she wouldn't get away with today. She could make herself ill by eating something poisonous. She could take an overdose of aspirin. But she didn't really want to die. It was only today she wanted to miss!

She put blotting-paper in her shoes, hoping against hope it would make her faint. She knew it had worked for others, but she had tried it before without success. Tara, horribly fit, had never fainted in her life. How she envied the girls who went down like flies during long assemblies, or caught chicken-pox and spent long weeks cosseted in the sanatorium.

She wasn't given long to brood. The gym must be prepared, the equipment laid out, the chairs put in position for the spectators.

After breakfast Miss Coles found her. 'Come along, Tara. We need someone with a bit of muscle behind them to arrange the mats. I hope your gym shoes are nice and white. We don't want to let the school down today of all days, do we?'

This sort of talk was alien to Tara. Caring nothing for Cranfield School where she was so unhappy, letting it down was the least of her worries. Letting herself down was something she did understand. She did it constantly, but the school?

Extraordinarily her fellow gymnasts were excited! There was a breathlessness about the warm-ups today that didn't come from the strenuous movements. Tara's heart grew heavier as the hours went by, bringing her nearer to the awful moment when she would have to perform, bulging out of her underwear, in front of a group of critical strangers.

They filled the hall with wafts of perfume and traces of damp fur coat which were out of place in the stark woodenness of the room. They chatted while they waited, and the girls, hidden from view in the changing-rooms, could hear them. It was hardly the kind of thing anybody would choose to watch, Tara knew. They were only there because they were proud of their daughters. They were only there because they had to be. She identified with them briefly before the self-pity came flooding back.

The opening crescendo made her jump. Out went the girls who were to give an introductory display of their own, the double-jointed, fearless ones. Tara stood, with her fingers plucking her lip, feeling fatter than she'd ever felt before.

'Wake up!' Miss Coles couldn't abide daydreamers. 'Your turn in a minute. Limber up, Tara! Limber up while you're waiting, like all the others!'

She was blinded to the sea of faces by the flood that pounded before her eyes. The music she was to keep time by ceased to exist, she was deafened by the booming sound coming from her ears. Automatically she followed the girl in front...Maxine

118

Haigue...she followed her actions, she trod in her dainty white footsteps. But Tara's weren't dainty no matter how hard she tried to move on the balls of her feet as Miss Coles had told her!

Tara Conway approached the horse. Its very shape appalled her. For her it was an instrument of torture. She galloped towards it, too fast. She leapt in the air too early. She crashed into its soggy sturdiness and hit it full on. She was winded, but not down.

The whole rhythm of the act was interrupted. Miss Coles blew her whistle and bawled, 'Carry on everybody. Carry on as if nothing has happened! Quick, quick, keep up!'

Even in their athletic postures Tara sensed a stiff-backed rejection from her peers. She had let them down. She had spoilt it all. Even if nothing else went wrong the display wasn't flawless now! But it wasn't her fault! No-one had listened to her. She'd told them she couldn't do it, often enough!

And then, out of the corner of one wild eye, she caught sight of her mother sitting in the front row wearing what must be a new hat. Her humiliation was complete, or she thought so, then... She must try! She must try harder! She would not let her mother down! She must have made a tremendous effort to get here today. She must have flown back from Cairo specially. And she'd done her best to look nice too...for Tara's sake!

Now she seemed to fumble and stumble over everything, but she kept going. There was only the dreaded 'waterfall' to go and then she'd be home and dry. Anyone could make one mistake! So she was the only one...well...it hadn't put her off completely, had it?

The box loomed in front of her like the broad leather back of an angry bull. It was ready for her! She was very aware of her mother's presence. She could even see the clip of her handbag where it shone under the harsh, gym lights. She could smell stale cigar-smoke and knew that Miss Coles wouldn't like that. Someone had been smoking in the gym...a crime above all crimes in this holy of holies.

After the near-fatal horse experience, Tara approached the box with caution. The terrible music became louder until it thundered in her ears. She was on the box! In a split second from now she would be standing on her hands on the edge, and everything behind her would be upside down. She felt herself begin to panic. She pushed herself on while the world spun around her. She was upright...upside down but upright. In a minute she would go over, land, and they would catch her. But no! She hadn't been forceful enough. She came down from her handstand onto her knees and had to try again. Girls were lining up behind her waiting for their turn. There was a blockage. Tara Conway was causing it! Miss Coles' face, red and waving about like a party balloon, loomed in her mind. She saw the lips purse. Up she went again...and again...and again, until finally, in a terrified frenzy, she pushed herself up with such force she went over too fast, the catchers missed her, and she landed on the ground flat on her back.

She stayed where she was, out of the way, allowing the others to pass her. But the music had stopped. They should have finished nicely minutes ago. They should be standing, red-faced, arms behind backs accepting their well-deserved applause. Instead, there was the sound of thumping, leaping bodies, and something else...

The ripple of laughter drenched her like the spray from a freak wave. It came from somewhere at the back of the audience and rose up, propelling itself forward with its own weight until it spread to those immediately around her. Even the girls were laughing. They had stopped what they were doing and given way to the dominance of the laughter. And everyone was staring...at her.

She lay on her back with her knees up like a beached whale...huge and monstrous...bigger and fatter than she had ever been in her life! Even her friend was laughing.

Tara sat up, brushing her hair from her eyes, and feeling to see if her pigtails were still tied. Her back hurt, her elbows were grazed, but otherwise she was fine.

Miss Coles, in her long, pleated shorts, was coming forward to address the audience. 'Ladies and gentlemen,' she said. She had to break into the retreating laughter. 'Parents...' Whether this was to cover any gaps or enlist their sympathy it was hard to tell. 'The girls have all done their best. As usual, it has been hard to foresee all possible variations to the planned programme...' The ripple of laughter started again and Tara felt her face burning. She deliberately kept her eyes from her mother. She couldn't bear to look at her.

It was over, and in neat lines they trotted back to the changing-rooms to the last of the half-hearted applause.

'Even Dr Rosewall, the chairman of governors, was there,' were the first words Miss Coles chose to berate her with. 'I'm speechless, Tara. I just don't know what to say! If I didn't know better I'd say you did it deliberately! You did your best not to take part, and because you couldn't get out of it you decided to ruin it. Was that it, Tara Conway?'

Nothing was further from the truth. Tara was speechless. What had happened was bad enough without this false accusation on top.

'You not only let all your friends down, you let the school down as well.' What friends? As far as she knew Tara only had one, and she had turned against her now. And as far as the school was concerned, well, she just didn't care. She had never felt more miserable in her life. And now she had to change and go and face her mother.

Nobody spoke to her in the changing-rooms. They turned their backs on her, agreeing with Miss Coles that she must have wrecked the performance on purpose.

'Nobody could be that stupid,' she heard Lorna Milne whisper, not too quietly.

'She's so ungainly.' That was Barbara Forrest, her friend. 'And she's so disgustingly fat!'

'I thought you were friends with her. You're always going round with her.' It was spoken as an accusation.

'Not really,' said Barbara Forrest. 'It's only when there's nobody else.'

Ten was a tender age for a broken heart, but it was Tara's third. The first had been when her father had died and she had been told that he wasn't coming back...ever. The second had been when she had parted from her mother three years ago, the 'Go and see if you can make some friends' episode.

Something had to happen. Something had to make her hard, cynical enough for survival in a cruel world. Over-sensitive. She read about people who were and wondered if that was what was wrong with her. But it didn't matter what the label was...it hurt too much.

You couldn't trust anybody. The only person you could depend on was yourself. She knew her own limits and in future she was going to insist on being listened to. She was never going to put herself in this last situation again.

Her mother was waiting for her in the dining-room where the parents were assembled for tea...homemade cakes and scones made by the domestic science classes. She looked so lonely standing there by herself. Her smartly suited back looked slim and vulnerable. She hadn't found anyone to talk to. A moment ago Tara had considered telling her the truth, explaining how she would rather go to a day-school, how unhappy she had always been at Cranfield. But how could she? Her mother's face lit up when she saw her. She wasn't expecting a load of bad news. She had enough problems as it was.

So Tara, before she went through the door, painted her face with a picture of cheerfulness and walked with an I'm OK swagger she never normally used.

'Messed it up again,' she said glibly, going out of her way to load up her plate...make it look as if nothing was wrong.

'At least everyone enjoyed themselves,' her mother said, brightly. 'It would have been very boring if you hadn't been there!'

'Yes, yes, I suppose it would.'

'Tell me about everything...how you are...what you've been doing. Oh, Tara, I miss you.'

Again, Tara nearly said, but held it back with the tears that would come later. Now was not the time.

Her mother looked lovely...happy, relaxed, much better than she'd been during the holidays. How come she had a child like me, Tara asked herself. I ought to be beautiful, slim and beautiful, like she is.

'I wanted to keep it a secret but I can't,' her mother told her eventually. 'I've found someone, Tara. Someone I'm very fond of. His name is Harry French, and if you agree, I'd like to bring him over to see you next time I come.' She added, 'He's looking forward to meeting you,' in a voice that made Tara feel younger than her age.

Immediately, Tara knew that this was the reason for her mother's unexpected arrival. She had wanted to sound her out. And it was important enough for her not to wait until the summer holidays.

126

She looked so very happy. She looked as if a dark veil had lifted from her eyes, and she was back to her old self again. She laughed and moved in ways that Tara had forgotten. She used little mannerisms that she used to use when her father was alive.

'I'd love to meet him. I can't wait. Yes, yes, bring him. Where is he now?'

'He's at home, Tara. He's staying with me for a while. I've put him in your old room...' She didn't want Tara to think they were sleeping together! 'In your old room...in your old room...' The words held the mocking ring of the laughing sailor or the fat lady at the fairground...the audience in the gym.

She couldn't keep it up. She knew she should have done but she just couldn't. And her mother, seeing the turmoil on her face, thought it was Harry French and that it was too soon to inflict a replacement father on her young daughter. And Tara was willing to let her believe anything rather than expose her own, flabby inadequacy.

That had been eighteen years ago. She'd kept them apart since then, although, strangely, nothing was ever said. She didn't know how. She didn't know why. It had just happened that way... She only knew that it was her fault.

She must be boring Pete to death. 'I've never told anyone before and I don't know why I'm telling you now... It's just something I really wanted to say...'

He put his arms round her, but this time she didn't mind. She held him, too. They were just good friends. And feeling safe, she cried. She cried as if her heart was breaking again.

And they stayed like that, needing each other, until the dawn started to break over the fourth day.

Nine

'Mum? I just thought I'd ring to find out how you were getting on.'

'Well I'm just fine! The last thing I was expecting was to hear from you. How is it up there, darling?'

'Grim, but the time's passing quite quickly. There's something nasty looming at the end, though. Some kind of performance. They invite the public in to watch...free! Joe says it's to try and inform people about the centre and show them what we do here is not just hard work but fun...and available to anyone who wants to get out of their car and use the countryside. I think I'd rather stick to my car. Do you remember the last time you watched me perform in public? A little less than successful, wasn't it?'

'When was that, darling?'

'Years ago. In that terrible gym display at Cranfield. You must remember!'

'No. I vaguely remember something...but not really. Anyway, who's this Joe person?'

A good question. Who was he? A man Tara couldn't get out of her mind...a man who dazzled her with his colours, inside and out...a blue-eyed, black-haired, brown-skinned man who liked to wear red, and who had managed, in the space of four days, to turn Tara's world upside down. 'Just one of the instructors here. How are the wedding arrangements coming along without me there to supervise? How's Harry?' As usual, when Tara started to talk about Harry, her mother's voice turned careful.

'Getting very excited about the whole thing. He's waited a long time for this. He's planning a secret honeymoon.'

If she hadn't spent the night talking to Pete, Tara would have quickly moved off the subject. This morning she didn't. 'How exciting! I'm beginning to look forward to the day so much! Did you get that hat you liked? Don't forget to order the drink this week, they said they needed three weeks' warning...'

'I've got it all under control. Tara, you sound...different. Is there anything wrong?'

'Nothing, except that I'm tired. I didn't get any sleep last night.'

'Oh? I didn't think it was that sort of course.'

'It's not, Mum.'

'Are you sure there's nothing wrong?'

'Quite sure. Now I must go. Give my love to Harry. Tell him...tell him from me it's about time he tied the knot.'

There was a brief silence on the other end, and then her mother said, still careful, 'I'll tell him. He'll be pleased you sound so...positive about everything. I'll see you at the weekend some time.'

'If I survive.' Tara gave a rueful smile.

'Oh you'll do that all right. Whatever else you are you're a survivor.'

Am I, she wondered as she put the phone down; or was that another of her mother's illusions based on Tara's competent performances?

Pete had gone to find Joe. He wanted to explain about last night. Tara had said he needn't bother, but he had insisted. 'I can't let him go around with that dreadful misconception of the situation,' he had told her. 'For my own sake, if not yours, I am going to tell him what happened.'

And Tara had already decided what she was going to do today. She was going to bed. She was going to be sensible for once in her life, tell them she was tired out, and sleep for as long as she wanted. If it read wrong on her report, then that was just too bad. She was so tired the air roared like lorries changing gear in her ears. It would be silly and dangerous for her to attempt anything that required her to be fully alert today.

She dreamed the peculiar, squashy dreams of the daytime sleeper, waking often and not knowing where she was or what was the time of day.

Then, suddenly, she was fully awake, eyes wide open and shaking off sleep. He was there. He had pulled up a chair and was sitting by her bed.

'How long have you been here?' She must look a fright...her face pillow-lined, her eyes heavy.

He smiled, and Tara swooned inside. When Joe smiled he used everything. There was nothing he held back. He looked too big for the chair, with his arms looped over the back of it and his legs splayed off the front.

'You'll get the sack,' she said. 'Coming into the women's dormitory like this when there's someone still in bed.'

'I've been watching you,' he said. 'I've been here about twenty minutes, just looking...'

'I thought you couldn't bear to sit still and do nothing,' she said. 'I thought you needed to get out there, to be active!'

He smiled again. 'Sometimes there are better things to do.'

She couldn't keep locked on his eyes. They were too powerful. She knew her breath had quickened, and her heart must be visible thudding away like that under the painfully-thin blanket.

'I thought I'd have a day off...'

'Pete came to talk to me.'

'Yes?'

'He explained about last night.'

'He said he was going to.'

'You were upset. By me?'

'Is that what Pete said?'

'That's what I'm asking you.'

Tara turned over and propped herself up on one arm. Her heavy brown hair, loose, fell forward and she hooked it back behind her ear.

'I don't know, Joe. I don't know what is going on inside me. I can't get things straight. I think last night was a mixture of lots of things.'

'We haven't got off to a very good start, have we?'

'It's not the start I'm worried about.' She had said too much, and wished she could have bitten those words back. Joe didn't miss anything, not an inflection, not a suggestion. He picked up on everything, and wouldn't let it go. He moved from the chair to the bed, to the space she had left between her propped up arm and her curled up legs. It was a tight fit. He was very close.

'Go on, explain,' he said softly.

'There's nothing to explain. I'm still a virgin, Joe. I'm twenty-eight, and still a virgin.' She waited for him to fall back, astounded.

'You're trembling.'

'I'm not.'

'Yes you are.' He laid his hand on her arm to soothe her. The gesture had the opposite effect on Tara.

'You shouldn't be here!'

'Don't you want me to be?'

She shook her head so her hair came loose, and then nodded.

'Where are the others today?'

'Do you really want to know?'

'I wouldn't have asked if I didn't.'

'Finding their way home with the aid of a compass. I dropped them off first thing this morning...miles from anywhere.'

'So no-one's likely to come in.'

Joe raised his eyebrows. 'No. We're quite alone.' He deliberately made his voice husky, playing the wolf!

A ripple of excitement ran through her, excitement tinged with apprehension. She dropped her eyes but he caught her chin and held up her face, watching. He let his fingers wander over the outline of her eyes, her cheeks, her nose, and down to her throat, stroking gently. She didn't move. She stayed as he'd positioned her, facing him, with her eyes closed.

He moved his hand to her shoulders, and hooked his finger gently under the flimsy strap of her nightdress...the one she'd soon realised was foolish to bring to a course like this. Everyone else wore pyjamas, or, like Aileen, flannelette! Hers was see-through, and she'd had a great deal of trouble in the open dormitory trying to preserve her decency.

He was close enough, now, for her to feel his breath on her cheeks. But he didn't kiss her. He stayed back far enough to watch the passage of his own fingers.

Nor did he speak, and there were flames in the silence between them. Tara breathed out heavily, and he stopped for a moment, and suddenly moved his hand down to her heart, passing her breast as he did so, his hand brushing her nipple.

She opened her eyes wide with surprise, and saw him smile again. He found her own hand and brought it down, with his, to feel the thudding there.

'Listen to your heart. I think it's a good thing we're alone,' he said. 'Don't you?'

So he knew. Tara sighed again and this time he kissed her. It was a fiercely passionate kiss, and she writhed under it, unable to keep her arms from moving up to his back and clasping him there. His body, unfamiliar to her, was firm and muscular, powerful and strong, and she let her hands explore his back with her fingers splayed to catch every sensation of it.

He moved away to study her again, to continue the run of his fingers. Tara had never experienced such desire. Her body was a fluid river, a bubbling, roaring volcanic flow of white-hot lava. And Joe seemed to know. He seemed to know what places to touch and where to linger. She was afraid he would go too far, and take her to a place from where he couldn't bring her back...a place she'd be lost for ever.

But as if he read her thoughts he murmured, 'Trust me,' as he slipped the straps off her shoulders and exposed her breasts to his narrowed blue eyes.

He whispered, 'Beautiful,' as she shivered, and cupped the two perfect domes loosely in his hands. Then he caressed her, kissed her, and her head fell back, allowing him free movement over her body. She wanted to be his...she wanted to be possessed by the man with the raven-black hair who seemed to know her own body better than she knew it herself.

She felt his hands follow the shape of her body, down to her waist and below. He pulled back the bedclothes and watched her movements through the sheen of her nightdress. He moved to her feet and kissed them, little, butterfly kisses that took her further into a delightful madness she hadn't known existed. His warm breath travelled higher, until he reached the source of her ecstasy, and with expert ease took her flying with him over the highest mountain peaks he could surely ever have climbed.

He held her. She was safe in his arms.

137

She had trusted him completely, she had revealed herself to him and he had not let her down. Everything was all right, all right, and he was telling her so.

'But you,' she sobbed. 'I'm all right, but what about you?'

'There's time for me,' he said softly. 'I'm in no hurry; now I know what's waiting for me, I would be happy to wait for ever. You're worth it. But don't take me literally,' he said. 'I'm not a patient man. Something tells me you need to take your time.'

She wanted to cover herself up. She wanted to hide away again but he wouldn't let her.

'What if someone comes?'

'No-one's going to come.'

'I feel embarrassed, lying here all open like this.'

'I have never seen anything so beautiful in my whole life, and you're talking about covering your body up as if it was something to be ashamed of.'

He meant what he said. It wasn't his words, although they were sincere, but his eyes told her he found her body wonderful. He drank her in as though she was a glass of expensive champagne.

He savoured her, he would have bound her in leather like a rare and precious book if he could have done...his eyes told her this. And yet...Tara, in the cold light of day, wanted to borrow Aileen's vast tent of flannelette and cover herself. She tried. He wouldn't let her.

'What if I was fat?'

'You're not fat.' He pinched, gently at her waist. 'Not a spare inch,' he said, his eyes crinkling at the edges in the way they had.

'But what if I was?'

'There'd be more of you for me to adore.'

'You sound like a Frenchman, like a practised lover. And you are, aren't you? You know exactly what you're doing, Joe. You must have had lots of experience.' It was something she couldn't bear to think about. The thought of him with other women made her feel sick. And yet she knew her feelings were unjustified.

He not only expected her to lie there brazenly like that, he expected her to eat naked, too. He went away to fetch some bread and pâté, some salad and a bottle of wine. As soon as he left she pulled up the covers. When he returned, balancing the tray and pretending to be a sexy French waiter to annoy her, he pulled them back again.

He picked the crumbs off her skin with his fingers. He balanced the cool wineglass on her breasts and held it there, placing a fleeting kiss on her lips as he did so. But being with him was so good. Their conversation, their laughter, their getting to know each other was so wonderful, there were times she forgot about her body and acted as if she was clothed.

'I'm glad you came here today,' she told him a little shyly because they'd stopped being serious.

'You've missed all that sleep you needed. I hope you won't try and make up for it tomorrow. I have to work tomorrow, and so do you!'

'You don't have to work at all,' she mocked him. 'You make enough money never to have to work again if you didn't want to. And I would far rather stay here and spend the day with you...' She played with his hair, winding the curly bits at his neck around her fingers.

'You little hussy,' he joked. 'All you can think about is sex! When I think how controlled I've been today, for your sake! We could have spent the last two hours really enjoying ourselves instead of messing about just talking.'

Tara laughed. Never, in her life before, could that accusation have been levelled at her. But it was quite true. She did want another day alone with him...a night would be better, a lifetime of nights. Now she sounded like Wanda! She was NORMAL. There was nothing wrong with her any more! She shook her head and laughed out loud with pure joy. She'd never known it could be like this.

He had to go. He had to take the van out to collect his team. He couldn't leave them stranded on a lonely Welsh hillside, no matter how much he wanted to stay with her, he said.

Tara felt bereft without him. She showered and dressed, taking extra care with her make-up, brushing her newly-washed hair until the burnished tresses shone with natural highlights. She stared at her eyes in the mirror. Darkly mysterious they were, and deeper, softer, more knowing...

Sure, confident of herself, she felt like singing as she went outside into the late afternoon wearing a fresh shirt and jeans.

Her secret warmed her. Every now and again she gave a private smile, letting her row of small, neat teeth show beneath her lips.

She wrote a card to Wanda, she'd promised she'd send one earlier, and sauntered over to the reception hut to post it. Nothing looked so bad...the pine-trees were extra bushy; the huts, after all, were quite attractive; basic, but right for the setting. And everywhere the scented smell of the pines was nothing less than exotic. She wondered why she'd never noticed before.

She hummed to herself as she pushed through the door making for the post-box. The receptionist was on the telephone. Tara had her hand in the box when she heard her say, 'No, there's nobody here just now. Alan and Carl are canoeing with their groups, Robin has taken his riding. And Joe has taken the van to Roewen. But he won't be back tonight because on Wednesdays he visits his wife...'

Black...black...everything went black. She must have posted the card because she came out without it. Like a sleep-walker she made her way back to the chalet, undressed, got into bed, and was there, huddled up under the covers when the others returned, full of their wonderful day!

'You'd have loved it,' said Aileen. 'There was nothing about it you couldn't have done with ease! It would have given you confidence! It would have done you the world of good. You should have come.'

If only Aileen didn't shout! There was no need. She could hear her very well. 'Yes, I should,' said Tara, from over blankets tight round her neck.

'You have to give him his due,' Aileen rambled on, pulling off her boots and replacing them with her dowdy old slippers. 'Joe's a clever instructor. He gets his timing exactly right, giving everyone a chance to shine at something they thought they couldn't do.'

'It's his job,' said Tara, pushing her face in her pillow, 'and he loves his work...you can tell.'

Ten

'The reason I didn't mention my wife is because she is my ex-wife, we are divorced, and apart from several shared business interests we do our level bests to see as little of each other as we possibly can, right?'

Tara, seething all evening and all night, had worked herself into a terrible state and had gone to confront him the next morning, seven-thirty in the morning to be exact. She had burst into his chalet, ignoring the various stages of undress of his fellow instructors, and the way they looked at each other in wry surprise.

'The girl on the phone didn't say ex-wife, she said wife!'

'Look, Tara.' Joe persuaded her to the door in his vest and pants. 'Do you want to see the legal papers? People talk like that! They don't expect to be listened into by someone who...'

'Someone who what? Go on, Joe?'

'Sometimes I think you are sick in the

144

head. You don't trust anyone. You expect to be used, to be hurt, and people who expect it like you do sometimes make it happen. I don't know what happened to you to make you like this, suspicious of everyone, but it must have been a hell of a traumatic event to have such consequences!'

There! He had said it! He found her disgusting, deep down he did! All of yesterday afternoon had been a performance!

'And yet you visit her every week? So regularly that the staff know where you're going to be without being told? And why does she live in Wales? If you're divorced why does she stay here?'

He was trying to contain his anger. But he looked wild, unshaven, and his voice was rough. 'When you visit by appointment like that, don't you think it sounds like a lack of something? And Tara, I didn't know, at this stage, that either of us had promised the other anything! If I'd wanted to spend the night making love to my ex-wife, heaven forbid, what would it be to you?'

'So you don't consider what we did yesterday afternoon to mean a thing?'

'Keep your voice down...' he glanced over his shoulder.

'Why the hell should I?'

'Because I say so.' His grip on her arms was hurting.

'You're embarrassed, aren't you? Making love to the clients is something you don't want to encourage among your staff! That's it, isn't it?' The grin on her face was set there. Her teeth were clenched, her body rigid. She wanted to stop but she couldn't. Something inside her drove her on.

He pushed her away in disgust. 'You make it sound revolting...as if we were two dogs making hay while the sun shone...'

'Wasn't that what it was for you?'

He shook his head as if she'd struck him. She didn't know why she was saying these things. She was hurting herself more than she was hurting Joe and yet she couldn't stop herself. She wanted to punish him...but for what? For making her feel complete for once in her life? For making her feel wonderful?

She wanted to punish him for making her trust him...for laying herself open to pain again...for her own vulnerability. And if she had stopped and thought about it she would have understood. But she didn't stop to think...she just careered straight ahead without looking.

'You used me!'

'Tara, I think you'd better go.'

'Oh yes. That would make it easier for you, wouldn't it? Get the hysterical woman out of your hair. Give you a chance to explain your behaviour to the others. Have a laugh...tell them all about what you did, another success for Joe Cornel, another conquest!'

'From what I remember of yesterday afternoon, it wasn't quite like that. Tara, you've said enough. Get out!' The look on his face was Mathew's. The tone of his voice was Mathew's, but much more cutting.

'Not until I've finished!'

'Finish then, and go.' His voice was terribly quiet, his eyes cold as ice.

She was limp and worn-out now, with nothing left to say. She remembered why she had come. 'I just wish you'd told me...about your wife, I mean,' she said lamely.

'Finished now?'

Tara nodded mutely and, knowing they were all watching, she left hut one and went out to face the desolate morning.

She'd been so terrified! Terrified that he had made a fool of her. But that was no excuse for the things she'd said. She'd believed he was trading on her vulnerability. She'd imagined he knew too much about her, and could whittle out her weaknesses and bend them to serve his own ends. What sort of person, then, did she consider him to be? A monster? A mind-reader? A wizard with long, pointed fingernails?

He was Joe Cornel and she loved him! But what now? In a moment she had blown it. She had thrown away the most precious experience of her life with a few hasty words, a butterfly off her hand. And then she had slapped her fists together and crushed it, broken its wings. Such happiness could never fly again.

'I know I'm alive when I'm out here, away from the humdrum pettiness of everyday life.' Joe was talking to Jeremy, but Tara overheard.

All day they had dealt in cold politeness, more painful than straightforward hostility, but easier, somehow.

'You've messed it up again then,' Pete

observed dryly, helping her to clip herself into her canoe.

'Yes. I have.'

'It'll be OK. There's enough time for things to change.'

'No, Pete,' said Tara. 'Not now.'

'Oh? It's that bad?'

'It's that bad!'

Pete nodded sadly in sympathy.

They were shooting the rapids. In Tara's book that's what they were doing, but Joe said it was a beginners' course. They had spent the morning practising rolling over and escaping in a still pool lower down the valley. She half hoped she'd have an accident so Joe would come and rescue her and she could make things right. But no such luck. She rounded the obstacles with her eyes closed against the stinging spray. The canoe had obviously done this before.

She suddenly seemed to have lost her fear. She didn't care what happened to her any more. She couldn't make a bigger fool of herself than she had already done today, and that fact seemed to make things easier. She rushed through the water, dabbing about hopelessly with her paddle, eager not to be a nuisance, eager to meld in with everybody else.

With Mathew it had been different. With Mathew she had had to face questions. Everyone who'd ever known them wanted to know why they were no longer together. If they didn't ask outright they asked their questions in roundabout ways. Four years is a long time. She'd known Joe for only four days.

At twenty-three, with no steady boyfriend, people had started looking at her as if she was peculiar. And that, she knew, was one of the reasons she had latched onto Mathew in the first place.

'You're made for each other,' people said, and Tara knew what they meant. They were both considered to be rather cold fish. They never held hands at parties, or smooched the night away to soft music. They didn't send romantic notes to each other, or drink wine by candlelight. And Tara was relieved because she didn't have to make an effort any more. She'd got her man! She was acceptable.

Then people started asking about the wedding. 'When's the big day?' Why was it always like that? There was no satisfying anybody. She knew that after that, the next thing would be, 'When's the baby due...you're not a proper family without a baby?' and so on. She was well aware that she was living to please other people, to try and placate everyone else. She must come into the scheme of things somewhere, but it was all a bit misty. Anyway, she liked Mathew. He didn't make too many demands...

When they went on holiday they always aimed to do something positive—archaeological digs which she loved—music workshops—touring Brontë country—and they booked separate rooms. Having Mathew around made it easier to socialise because they were a pair and he could talk to anyone quite happily. Tara just tagged along behind him. In fact, Mathew was better with people he didn't know...because he did have a tendency to repeat the same old stories, tell the same jokes. He had a repertoire, and after he'd exhausted it he sometimes seemed to be quite frighteningly empty!

Of course they used to kiss...and cuddle. But it didn't go further than that. Mathew was an old-fashioned sort of man in most ways...so were his parents. And Tara knew they would live the same sort of life as they did...two children...mortgage...car...dog...

She would be expected to stay at home and keep the house nice. Not that there was anything wrong with that, but Tara was overpowered by the stifling respectability of it all. Respectability, responsibility, decency, it dominated their lives. What other people said mattered.

Sometimes she wanted to scream and go wild. Something was wrong, but she did nothing to end it.

She flirted at a party with a man whose name was of no consequence. She enjoyed that party! She drank too much, and she wasn't ready to go home when Mathew was. She danced on, draping herself over her new-found friend, accepting his kisses to her neck and arms, losing herself in the music. She yearned...oh she yearned...she desired...she wanted...

When she cried on her partner he asked her why. She shook her head and told him she honestly didn't know.

Mathew watched, a drink in his hand. She watched as he became moodily black. Why? He wouldn't want to do this. Why did he care if she did? He must accept, surely, that they were different people, that she had needs, too, and they weren't necessarily the same as his.

He was quiet in the taxi going home. Tara was giggly and bubbly and guilt-ridden. As the effects of the alcohol wore off, the world became colder and starker, reality a place where she didn't want to be.

He came in for a coffee. Most times he didn't. He was still sulking. 'You enjoyed yourself tonight,' he said, sounding like a courtroom lawyer.

Tara filled the kettle and pushed past him into the sitting-room to light the gas fire, her lips held tightly together. She didn't want to say the things she was feeling...but he would make her if he didn't stop looking at her like that.

'After we're married do you still intend to behave in this way?'

His words lingered in the atmosphere like a wisp of stale smoke. She wanted to flap them away with her hand or open a window to let them out. She left him to fetch the coffee. Her hand shook as she carried the tray back into the room and she slopped some of the liquid onto the saucers.

He was a tweedy man, a jacket and pipe man, a comfortable man. Or she'd always thought him so. His ideas were comfortable, too, his views on life set. They were the same views as those held by his mother. He didn't like anybody, and normally she listened placidly while he belittled the behaviour of most other people who failed to match him in common sense, wit and prospects. He never gave an inch. He never realised that there were reasons for people's behaviour, reasons very often out of their control.

She was unreasonably angry with him. Unable to excuse herself for her unusual behaviour, she had to take it out on somebody. It was unfair. She knew what Mathew was like. It was unfair of her to turn on him just because she wasn't in the mood to put up with him. She seemed to be seeing him clearly for the first time...with his little bald patch already and his over-large, white hands. Cruel...you're being too cruel...the bells of warning rang, but they weren't loud enough.

'When we are married I shall behave exactly as I see fit, Mathew. I don't intend to be told how...'

'What if I'd behaved as you did? How would you be feeling?' It was a fair question. With a shock, she realised she wouldn't mind at all.

'But you wouldn't, would you Mathew? You have too much self-control...'

'You little whore!' That's when he shot out of his chair and came to stand behind her by the fireplace, circling her with his arms and thrusting his hand inside her blouse.

She swung round to face him. 'How dare you!'

'I'm only taking what's mine.'

'Not yet, it isn't...'

'I'm taking it before you give it to somebody else.'

'It? It?' she snarled like a dog, baring her teeth at him. 'You talk about me as if I'm a rubber doll.'

He pushed her down onto the sofa, clamping his mouth so tightly onto hers that his teeth bruised her lips. 'You egg me on and then you back off,' he said. 'If you can go that far at a party you can go all the way with me!'

'Mathew!' She kept her voice controlled. He was trying to take off her blouse. 'I'm sorry. I didn't mean to behave like that. I'm not really like that. I don't know what came over me.' But he didn't seem to hear her. His voice was unsteady and the freckles under his skin stood out as he mauled her. 'I didn't think you were that kind of girl,' he was saying, over and over again. 'You're dirt, that's all you are, dirt!'

'Mathew!' she shouted above his mumblings. 'Stop this now!'

'You don't mean it. This is what you want.'

'It is not what I want. Stop it, this instant!'

He pushed her away, disgusted, and stood over her. 'I've thought this for a long time now,' he said. 'And I'm going to tell you exactly what I think of you. You are a frigid bitch, and under all that superficial finery you are nothing but a whore! There is something the matter with you. I don't know what it is but there is something wrong...'

'Because I don't want to make love to you against my will?' Tara raised her voice to match his. 'And how can I be a frigid bitch and a whore at the same time? That doesn't make any sense, Mathew, it really doesn't.'

'My mother was right,' he said.

'What do you mean, your mother was right?'

'She always said you were..."common,

156

unsubtle" were her words, but common will do me. But I thought I could change that in you. I thought I could mould you, make something of you...'

'Mathew. You never seemed to want to take our physical relationship very far before.' Her words were even and considered.

'That sort of thing should be reserved for the bedroom,' he said stiffly. 'And certainly not before marriage.'

'And we've been engaged for two years. I've known you for four.'

'It doesn't matter. We're not animals. We don't have to perform like everyone else does. And I thought you felt the same way, until tonight.'

'Nothing has changed.'

'Oh yes it has. Oh yes it has.' He was being dramatic, now, pulling himself up to his full height, pulling his stomach in. 'You've shown yourself in your true light. Women!' he said. 'They're all whores underneath!' And he turned and left the room, with the presence of mind to throw the spare keys down on the sofa beside her. Gaping up at him, she watched him bang the door and disappear onto the lighted steps outside.

Feeling wobbly, she crossed the room in the half-light and pulled back the curtain so she could see him go. She had to experience as much of this as she could...it was her punishment. She listened as his footsteps, quick and angry, grew fainter but didn't slow or turn round. She felt dirty. She felt dirty and sick. What was wrong with her? She wanted something...but she didn't want Mathew. Of that she was sad but certain.

Now, too late, she knew who she wanted, but she could not take back the words she'd said to Joe.

She watched him now as Simon and Jeremy helped him strap the canoes on the top of the van. He gave one of his slow smiles, not to her. He made a quick remark, the others laughed. All his movements seemed effortless. He had a boundless energy. Cool in all circumstances. She should have known he'd have been married. No-one as attractive as Joe Cornel could reach his thirties unmarried. She was jealous! Tara was jealous of his wife, divorced or not.

But calm now, she believed what he'd told her. He hadn't been taking advantage of her or having a bit of fun on the side. That was a product of her own imagination, caused by a terror of being ridiculed.

He wasn't the sort of man to do that. And he wasn't the sort of man to treat her wild accusations lightly, either. How could she make it right? Or had she gone too far?

Eleven

Where could she go where she'd be alone? Where would she find peace and quiet and be left to her own devices?

'Come into Bangor with the rest of us,' said Emma. 'Don't go off moping on your own.'

'I'm not moping,' Tara smiled brightly. 'See? I'm happy, happy, happy!'

'You're lying,' said Aileen. 'You're like the skeleton at the feast. Come with us. We'll cheer you up. There are plenty more fish in the sea, believe me!'

What did Aileen know about it, cheerful Aileen with all her trite clichés? She looked as if she'd never suffered in her life. And then Tara remembered she normally tried to look like that. The difference between them was that Aileen was succeeding while she...

'One more day to go,' chanted Pete. 'One more day of sorrow.' And then, seeing Tara's face, he said, 'Sorry. Didn't mean to be flippant.'

160

If she went with them she'd throw a dampener on their morning off. A morning of freedom! A morning for shopping, resting, swimming, doing whatever you felt like. Tara waved them off. They were going in Pete's car. They'd saved a place for her. They were concerned for her.

Tara hadn't admitted it to herself yet, but she planned to hang around and see what Joe was doing. She didn't want to leave the centre in case she bumped into him and then he'd have to say something... The trouble with the course was that there were always so many people around. They saw each other...but not to talk to...not as Tara wanted to talk. And Joe appeared to be ignoring her.

She was going to apologise and try to explain. She didn't know how yet, but she was going to try. She'd done nothing else but ponder the problem. He was a reasonable man, he would listen to her. They had been close. He was attracted to her, she hadn't imagined that. Surely all was not lost?

When most people had gone, certainly all her group, she chose a meandering route that would take her near chalet one. It was out of her way, but she strolled casually along as if she had no plan in mind. As she got nearer her heart beat faster. She had dug out the clothes she had worn on the second day...the day he had first kissed her up by the lake. Maybe there was something about that blue and white striped shirt that had attracted him then...and it might again.

She heard his voice and her heart nearly stopped. She coloured so profusely she thought she would overheat and explode. And worse than that, she grew...she grew and she grew like Jack's beanstalk, except she grew wide as well as tall. She felt huge, an uncontrolled, gigantic piece of plasma, big and unwieldy, spreading out across the path. Every nerve was on edge as she waited, churning over in her mind what she might say. As if she hadn't already rehearsed a thousand possible conversations.

She turned the corner and the three of them were coming towards her, Joe, an instructor she knew as Robin, and another called Carl. They had all been witnesses to yesterday's outburst. She felt foolish immediately. It was blatantly obvious that she was looking for him. She felt like a schoolgirl hanging around the bicycle-shed waiting for a prefect, and just as gauche!

Although they were deep in conversation, Joe looked up and saw her. She couldn't read his expression—not from here—but his pace didn't alter, nor did the pattern of their talking. Something amused them. Could it be her? No, she was paranoid. They'd been laughing before they'd even seen her.

She wished, now, that she could disappear, call up a genie and hide in his lamp. She quickened her walk, making it seem that she was in a hurry with somewhere definite to go.

If she didn't speak now they'd go by, and she'd have lost her opportunity. She was spurred on by a sudden bravery, but calling out to him was the lesser of the evils. Her alternative was to mope about all morning in the depths of this utter misery until she saw him again.

'Joe...'

They were level with her when she spoke. They fanned out to let her pass. They were four steps on when her call registered. The others walked politely on, pairing together and saying something she couldn't hear.

Joe stopped and turned round, eyebrows

raised as if nothing was more unexpected. He wore blue today, a blue that accentuated his eyes. He wore a loosely-knitted jumper over faded denim jeans. His sleeves were part rolled up, revealing tanned forearms under bright, white shirt-sleeves.

Head bowed, Tara approached him, playing with her fingers, all her lines forgotten.

He wasn't going to help. He wasn't saying a word.

'Joe, I just wanted to say...' she gulped.

'I thought you were going out this morning?'

'No. I...'

'I can't wait now, I'm in a hurry. I'll catch you later.'

And he was gone. He'd been so close she'd felt the air move as he turned and left her.

She felt like a blob of spilt ice-cream melting there on the path, all that monstrous hugeness dribbling away to nothing. Soon she'd disappear completely. They were talking together as if nothing had happened. Was it about her? She heard Joe laugh as they went round the corner of the reception hut and out of sight. She heard the engine of the Range

Rover. She heard tyres crunch gravel as the car reversed, went forward and off down the drive.

And then her own footsteps sounded, very slow and solitary.

She took cover in the local library. This was an old ruse of Tara's going back to her schooldays.

She walked there. She didn't trust herself in the Morgan. Through the doors and she was at home. It could have been the school library. That familiar sense of peace that assailed her there, peace she could gulp like a drink. That fresh but musty smell of print...she always felt she wanted to lick it... the high shelves where you could disappear as you stretched and stooped to choose...in this room you could choose to go anywhere. It was Tara's patch of sky through which she could soar to many heavens.

She went to the first row, started at the A's, still with her mind elsewhere, still in a dream. She reached the B's without seeing anything. Mechanically she took books out just for the pleasure of it, and put them back neatly with a pat. CORNEL...JOSEPH. The name leapt out and hit her between the eyes. She stopped breathing. A common name, be sensible, there must be thousands of Joseph Cornels. But she had to look.

'THE ANT AND THE MOUNTAIN,' and there was a picture of Joe just inside the front. With the book open she felt her way to a table and sank onto a chair, unable to take her eyes from the picture. Joe was leading a Himalayan expedition. It was taken in snow, there was ice on his eyebrows, and he held two climbing-sticks in his hands. Underneath was a homely reproduced photograph. It was of a small boy in hospital, wearing pyjamas. He, also, was holding two sticks in his hands.

'Disabilities come in all shapes and sizes. We've all got them. The worst are those you cannot see. A disability is something that stops you doing what you want to...but it's easy to turn it round and say you don't want something just because you think you can't have it.'

Three hours later Tara walked back to the centre lost in her thoughts.

'I was told a story when I was little. It was about an ant that couldn't climb a mountain. He told everyone he didn't want

166

to. Nasty places, mountains, he would say, especially to those, like the eagles, who lived there. Nasty, ugly, barren places. I'm glad I can't get up there...what would anyone want to go up a mountain for, I ask you. Give me a nice, warm kitchen cupboard any day, and a jar of syrup...'

Tara frowned. It happened with people, too. At school she had most despised those she'd have liked to be friends with but couldn't be... or felt she couldn't.

'I was lucky,' Joe had written. 'I wasn't afraid of dying because I grew up with death so close to me. In a way it became a childhood friend, because I knew that if the pain became too bad, if something went too badly wrong, death was there. I wouldn't just endlessly suffer. I learned early that there are far worse things in life than death.'

He'd had polio. Nobody, these days, gets polio. Yes they do, Joe assured her in his book, and it wasn't nice.

'People treated me as if I was stupid, not just handicapped. They didn't expect anything of me, in fact they steered me away from difficulties, telling me not to tax myself too much, thinking I'd get frustrated and angry if I couldn't do things. And I did! All the time!'

With every step Tara grew more ashamed of herself. Here she was, healthy, able and miserable as sin...handicapped for ever over something as trivial as an unhappy childhood. Joe had spent four years in hospital. Most of them in pain. After that he'd gone to school on crutches. He'd been behind with his schoolwork, stuck in a lower class with children younger than him...yet she hadn't been able to discover one word of self-pity in the whole book. On the contrary, he considered himself luckier than other people! His experiences had given him the will, he said, to succeed.

Perhaps people had been extra nice to him because he was a cripple? She'd read the next few chapters with that hope. Perhaps he didn't know what it was like to be ostracised by his peers.

She was disappointed. He knew very well what that was like. He spent a whole chapter on it and she'd ended up feeling sorry for them, not him! 'We're all so frightened of being grouped with the outsider,' he wrote. 'Something about them, we fear, will wipe off on ourselves, and then we'll be pariahs, too. It's a measure,' he said, 'of our insecurity, and the crueller we are, the more frightened. It's a vicious circle.'

Tara groaned. He wrote about how he had built up his business. Anyone could do it, he said, if they wanted to badly enough. He didn't say the same of the mountains. He said that took nerve, and that some people lacked confidence...

He didn't talk much about his marriage, but there was a picture of his wife, Anna, posing outside a ski lodge. There were lots of pictures. Anna was classically beautiful, with heavy, black hair, a swan-like neck and perfect features. In the photograph Tara stared at with such curiosity, she wore a full-length shaggy fur coat, high black boots and a cossack hat. She looked like a model. Tara wondered if capturing Anna had been something to do with Joe's need to prove himself...if you could end up married to a siren like that, you had surely proved your manhood to the world.

She hadn't joined the library in order to take the book out. She hadn't wanted anyone to know she'd read it. Her reasons for this were confused. But she knew that although it was a book, and available to anybody, for her there had been something private about it. Most of the time she had experienced the feeling that Joe was talking directly to her, in confidence, and nobody else. He had that way of writing.

Knowing what she now knew, Tara felt she was in a difficult position, although clearly Joe didn't mind anybody reading about his past. She felt embarrassed, as if she had discovered a secret about him. She assumed he would not want her to know. Why? Tara shook her head, baffled by her own question. Because she was ashamed of her past unhappiness and thought it reflected badly on her character, why should Joe be?

The others were back and having lunch when Tara arrived. There was no sign of Joe and his friends.

Aileen had bought herself a track suit. Everyone was admiring it.

'I'm not going to let myself get sloppy again,' she was saying. 'I'm going to take up squash when I get home.'

'What about you, Tara?' Jenny turned round to smile. 'What are you going to do to keep fit?'

Tara, knowing she was joking, said, 'I'm going to take the roof of my car off more often.'

'Huh! With all the fumes in London, you'll end up with damaged lungs.'

Except for one day it was all over. People were already thinking in terms of going home. Tara realised, with a sudden pang, that she didn't like the thought of leaving them all, of never seeing them again. They had grown extraordinarily close. She was fond of them.

Emma, catching her thoughts, said, 'I think we should have a reunion.'

'It never works,' said Pete. 'People sound keen, but when the time comes they don't want to bother. We'll soon forget we ever came here. It will be a vague memory. A year from now and we won't remember each other's names.'

'Don't be so depressing, Pete,' said Emma, digging into a plateful of vinegary chips. 'I won't forget, anyway.'

'You've got a reason for remembering,' said Aileen. 'You nearly came to grief on a cliff face. The rest of us haven't.'

She didn't see Tara look quickly down at her hands. She knew she would never forget this week. She would remember everybody sitting round this table, their every feature, their every gesture, because they were all part of the backcloth of her affair with Joe...

No! They were much, much more than that. She wanted a reunion, too, and she remembered the words in Joe's book, you only had to want something badly enough to make it happen.

'I'll take a list of names and addresses before I go,' she heard herself saying. 'And I'll keep in touch with all of you and arrange something next year. I want to know what happens to you...I want to see you all again.' She was pleased she'd said it. By the look on their faces they all were.

Joe came in. He affected them all in different ways. He immediately had their attention. He didn't have to do anything, say anything, just by being there he assumed leadership.

'When you're ready we're going to have a look at the adventure course,' he said, humour never far from his voice. 'We've got a performance to do tomorrow, and we ought to get a bit of practice in. I'll be there in a minute...all the groups are taking part in this so there'll be fifty of us altogether.' He scanned the group quickly with his vital eyes. 'Tara,' he said, in front of everybody. 'Did you want to see me?'

Tara, not expecting this, flushed. 'No...' she said, quailing under his gaze. 'No, Joe, it was nothing.'

He nodded, joked about something else with Jeremy, and left the room with Emma, full of questions, trailing along behind him.

Twelve

Friday. The day of the display! When she woke up that old monster was squeezing her chest again.

And she ached from missing Joe. All last evening she'd made herself available, taking herself off on her own to stand or sit in odd places...places where Joe might find her. He wasn't looking. He was busy. He was involved. He was happy. He seemed to have forgotten there had, ever been anything between them. Perhaps there hadn't.

'OK! That's it! You've moped around for long enough. Pull out of it, Tara! You're trailing around like a lovesick teenager. When you walk like that, when you set your face to miserable, it makes you feel worse inside.'

'Aileen, how do you know?'

'Everyone knows. Broken hearts aren't your prerogative, Tara. Ask anyone here, they know how you feel. But you've just got to try, somehow. You mustn't let yourself go with it. Fight it!'

'Why won't he talk to me?'

'Perhaps he hasn't got anything to say. Perhaps he's embarrassed. I don't know why he won't talk to you. But you've tried to get him on his own. He obviously doesn't want you to. Now it's time you fought back!'

'Against what?'

'Against your own self-destruction. Now come on!' Aileen pulled her up, supervised her dressing and dragged her along to have breakfast.

Tara told Aileen about the book.

'I know. I read it ages ago. He set up this centre as a result of the response he got...all those frightened people who wanted to achieve great things but were too afraid.'

'How did it get to be a training scheme for executives? Bit of a come-down, isn't it?'

Aileen reached for the toast. 'There are only two courses of this kind during the year. He openly admits he charges five times as much for these, and they help to pay for people who can't afford the normal charges.'

'How mercenary of him!'

Aileen looked at her quizzically. 'If it helps to get him out of your system to put him down...then that's just fine. Do it! But to be fair to him, he believes that people under stress at work, us presumably, have fears as well, and as much right to work on them as anybody else in order to survive.'

Tara groaned. 'I don't mean to be nasty.'

'No, go on, be as nasty as you like. It might help, and something's got to!'

'I'm not looking forward to negotiating that high rope bridge in the tree-tops.' Pete was trying to take Tara's mind off her problems. They all were. They seemed to have made some pact...or was it her imagination? They wouldn't allow her to fall back into her own thoughts. They wouldn't allow her to back away from the conversation. They kept addressing her, asking her questions, including her in the general interaction. So for their sakes she tried...hard...

'Or the wall,' Emma chipped in. 'I don't know how I'm going to climb that with only that flimsy rope to help me.'

Tara had pushed the day's activity to the back of her mind. It wasn't her main worry. She couldn't cope with it. She knew she would fail...success didn't come into the equation. All she could do was hope she wouldn't make such a clown of herself as she had back at Cranfield... She'd been dreading today all week, since she'd been told about it. But if she pulled out, Joe might think the action was directed at him and she didn't want that. She was trapped.

She had considered getting herself stuck in the underground pipe they had to crawl through, but she didn't want to cause a fuss or spoil the team's chances of winning. The five teams were competing against each other in a friendly sort of way. And Tara didn't want to let the A team down. She frowned...how had she come to think this way? It wasn't like her at all.

Joe came in to breakfast late and sat with Carl and Robin. When he was in the room Tara stiffened from the tension in the air. She pretended not to watch him but she did...whenever she got the opportunity. Why was he always flanked by those two? Why was he never alone? Was he doing it deliberately to keep her at bay? How awful! She squirmed.

'He's easy to fall in love with, isn't

he?' Tara wished Emma wouldn't talk like that. Was she in love with him, too? Was everyone secretly in love with him? jealousy flared again. It hurt.

'It's his muscly thighs and his hairy legs,' Jenny joked.

'No,' Emma mused. 'There's a brooding kind of mystery about him, as if he knows many things. I bet he'd make a wonderful lover! Look at his eyes!'

If they thought this trivialising helped, they were wrong. It only made Tara more abjectly miserable.

During the morning holidaymakers trickled in with their flasks and sandwiches. They took up positions on the sunny banks that flanked the adventure course. They spread their rugs out on the ground, they tethered their dogs to trees. Their children played on the safer types of obstacles. Tara had seen the notice on the great stone gateposts on her journey back from the library yesterday.

'Come and join us,' it had said, 'Friday afternoon. Adventure course. Watch the teams compete. Test yourselves. Swim in the pool. Picnic on the rocks. Canteen available.' She felt like a performing chimp. The more the cars came drifting in, the more surprised she was. She hadn't expected so many people. Why would they come here when they could be on the beach? Personally, she couldn't imagine coming to watch anything more dreadful.

The more people who came and dotted themselves colourfully on the grass, the more the carnival atmosphere seemed to grow. But so did the tension. Two of the instructors were working with the children...there was a course specially for them underneath the real one! It looked far more suitable for her, Tara thought. She might have been able to cope with that.

And others had made themselves at home by the side of the pool, sunning themselves on their towels while drowsily observing the antics of those more active among them. They were all so relaxed! Clearly this was because they weren't under any compulsion to take part in anything...they could come and go as they pleased.

'It's not meant to be a fraught sort of occasion,' Joe was saying to Pete. 'It's supposed to be fun...you know...easy going...'

Pete's face reflected the exact opposite of those things. It grew long and ponderous, wanting to know every detail of what they were meant to be doing. 'That's easy for you to say. We're the ones who have to make spectacles of ourselves.'

'And learn that it doesn't really matter,' said Joe. 'That's what's important for you to realise!'

Joe caught Tara's eyes and looked quickly away. He is avoiding me, she thought. He doesn't want to know. And her heart sank, heavy and solid as a doughy ball.

They ate ice-creams as they read the task assigned to each team. Every piece of that dire equipment was to be used by every member of every group. Tara didn't trouble to read it too carefully. Someone would tell her what to do and where to go when the time came. Until then it was best she didn't know.

'It's quite simple really,' said Simon, all keen. 'Basically all we've got to do is get an injured person from A to B without allowing the body to touch the ground.'

'I'll be the injured person,' Tara was quick to say.

Simon gave a withering sigh. 'It's a dummy,' he said reproachfully. 'We need every member of the team...we can't carry passengers.' How she loathed this sort of talk! Jeremy and Simon would be far more successful on their own. In real life you wouldn't use ten people to get a body home! It was all so silly!

By the time they had finished discussing the ins and outs of the problem, even Tara was concerned about the feelings of the faceless casualty. No, they couldn't dangle it from ropes tied to its legs...no, they couldn't float it across the water on its own. They had to pretend it was a real person...in pain...wounded...needing their help.

They had to devise their own plan. They weren't allowed to copy other people's. To stop them cheating, they had to write down and show how they aimed to carry out the task before they started.

They handed in their piece of paper and sat down to watch. They were going third...the positions had been pulled out of a hat. We might as well be children playing party games, Tara thought disconsolately. It's pathetic!

Her hands were wet and they shook as she took up her position in something like a crow's nest, high above the ground...her hands, and every other part of her. She had climbed a rope-ladder to get there. She had crossed a rickety bridge, and trundled breathlessly across a trampoline. Now, with a beating heart, she waited for the body to arrive on its make-shift stretcher, swung at her on ropes from a great height. She had to catch it, and having strapped herself to the rope, she had to swing down to the ground, arriving so that she and the body were safely ready for the next leg of their hair-raising journey. It was one of the easiest manoeuvres, that's why she'd been given it. All she had to do was let go...and let herself swing.

Tara kept her eyes closed so she couldn't see the ground. Surely this was training for the marines? She heard the body come whistling through the trees. She leaned forward and opened her arms. She missed it. It came again. She wasn't ready. Oh God oh God oh God...she was letting everybody down...she was messing it up again.

She was a little girl again, back in the gym at Cranfield, and just as hopelessly ungainly. She couldn't make her body *move properly*. The wind in the leaves began to sound like laughter...wave upon wave of rustling, tinkling laughter...

How had Simon and Clive got here? She hadn't time to wonder. She was on the rope and flying...safely to the ground. The landing was soft, the pulleys held. She stood there shaking, forgetting what it was she had to do next. She gaped at the audience. They gaped back.

Paul grasped her arm. What was he doing here? He helped her wheel the body to the river where the punt was waiting. Emma and Pete were on it already, calling encouragement. Over the river they went, careful to keep the body bone-dry, up the other side and to the wall.

Everything happened so quickly that outside her own small, puffing dimension the world became a blur. Tara stopped at the bottom and stared up at the sheerness of the wall in awe. Jeremy was up at the top, pulling. Simon and Paul hauled at the stretcher. It inched its way up the wall, dozens of hands helping it along the way. Everyone but herself was on the wall. Even Pete and Emma were halfway up.

They left the body on the top and came for her. In no time she was astride the top looking down. Jenny and Aileen helped her down, but, she realised with amazement, she was doing most of the work herself!

Now she had to crawl under the nets, holding them up so that Jeremy and Simon could pull the stretcher along without getting stuck. She did it with ease...nothing to it...and she was quick!

They were up in the trees again...Tara with her eyes closed. They had climbed a steep ramp to get here, and now they had to cross the thin rope bridge over what had to be a chasm far below. The air sung in her ears. She felt herself swaying, and she wasn't on the bridge yet! They had to form a line across it. The body was to be passed along by the first two to the second two and so on. Tara stepped out onto the bridge and felt it give. She couldn't do this...she just couldn't.

'I can't do this,' said Emma, who always looked so capable and athletic. 'There's nothing on earth going to make me do this.'

'Come with me,' said Tara. 'As I said before, I'm not afraid of heights.' And she stepped out over the void, taking Emma's hand.

'I've got my eyes closed,' said Emma. 'I can't bear to open them.'

'Don't worry,' said Tara. 'I can see for both of us.' And when she looked she saw they weren't very high...not really...not as she'd imagined they were.

The others were making it easy for her. Whatever she did they were there, watching, helping, making sure she wasn't afraid. There was nothing she could do to make a fool of herself today. They weren't going to let her! It was a good feeling...so good she started to lose her fear. And she trusted them completely. When hands were held out she took them. When voices told her where to put her feet, she followed them. They were on her side! They were not about to let her down!

Before she knew it, it was over, and she was laughing, exhausted, with the rest, wiping her hands free of sweat, clearing the sticky hair from her face.

'That was great!' She took great gulping breaths of fresh air.

'Pardon? Did I hear you correctly?' Emma was laughing, too, a weak, tired giggle. 'I thought I'd never get down from that rope...'

'And the ladder was exhausting...near the top...'

'I nearly dropped the stretcher when we were unloading it off the punt.'

Everyone was breathless, dishevelled, and

exhausted. They spoke in quick bursts. It was the only way.

'You were brilliant,' Jeremy told Tara. 'Absolutely brilliant.'

'I wasn't! It was you...you all helped me. Was it planned?'

'Well Pete did let out earlier in the day a little story about your experiences in one particular gym...'

Tara crumpled under surprised laughter. 'Pete! That was a confidence!'

'I considered it better broken,' he said, leaning forward, hands on knees, gasping to get his breath back.

These people were all wonderful. Tara was filled with a furious, protective love towards them all. They hadn't cared whether they won or lost. They had cared about each individual member of their group. That's what had mattered. It was as far away from her experience at Cranfield as the sun was from the moon... She wished Miss Coles could have seen her today! She wouldn't have believed it was the same person! With a sudden sadness, Tara wondered if Miss Coles was still there, doing the same thing to other children...

The audience approved. They were clapping enthusiastically. And Tara heard

186

someone say, 'Weren't they good? I'd never have the nerve...'

She couldn't remember a time when she'd ever felt better about herself, and feeling as she did, she looked wonderful, too. Her eyes sparkled and her personality bubbled. She turned round, lifting the hair from her neck to cool herself, and saw Joe standing alone on a rock above the waterfall.

Even though he was just a silhouette against the sky, she couldn't mistake him. All the goodness drained away. She was left limp and aching again...she wanted him so badly. But she wasn't going to let anyone know. She wasn't going to spoil the atmosphere for anyone else. They were out to have a good time and she was going to help them!

They swam in the pool, they sunbathed. They picnicked under the trees and Aileen drank too much wine. In other circumstances, the dreaded test over, Tara would have thoroughly enjoyed herself.

'It's 'cos I'm happy,' Aileen said woozily. 'I only get tipsy when I'm really happy.'

It was scorching hot again, hot as it had been on the day they arrived. By the time the last group had finished performing it was late afternoon, and the heat was debilitating.

'Let's organise a party tonight,' Pete suggested from the shade of his tree. 'We'll go and get some bottles and some bits to eat. We can hold it in our hut...Paul's got a tape-recorder and...'

'I've got hundreds of tapes in my car,' Jeremy said.

'What about the other groups?'

'Anyone can come,' said Pete, 'as long as they bring their own booze.'

'It feels as if we're being naughty,' said Emma. And she was right. They'd been treated a little like youngsters all week...just being there had made them feel like that, obeying orders, following a routine, assessment at the end of it just like school reports. This was something they wanted to organise for themselves, a kind of mini-revolution.

Tara had planned to hide away early tonight, take out her grief and look at it, nurse it all by herself. Now she would really be tested. Could she keep up this façade? Would they notice if she left? Would she spoil things?

There was no time to brood. They tore

down to the local off-licence before it closed. They bought bread and cheese and nibbly things, and remembered a corkscrew at the last moment.

She wanted to ask if the instructors would be invited but didn't like to in case she sounded lovelorn.

This last night could have been so different, she kept saying to herself. It was her own fault things were as they were. She had brought this on herself.

But had she? What could a person like Joe Cornel possibly want with her? He could have his pick of anyone. He had been through the mire and come out the other end with flying colours...not like her. He had felt sorry for her, she convinced herself. He had not meant her to feel so strongly about him, and when he realised what a mistake he had made he had backed off...as anyone would...

It would, she thought sadly to herself, have happened anyway. He would have found me out in the end.

Thirteen

Tara dressed to kill.

You could be as successful as you liked, you could achieve things you never thought possible, you could be surrounded by supportive friends, but if you'd lost the man you loved nothing counted. And her clothes and her make-up acted as armour...armour against that truth. She looked radiant tonight.

Aileen, needle-sharp, looked at her as she came through the door, and registered approval.

They'd pushed the beds to the far end of the room and piled them on top of each other. They'd attempted to decorate the spartan place with bits of greenery that had gone limp in the heat. All the windows were open, and from here you could just hear the river running coolly in the distance. Night bugs, attracted by the light, grouped in clouds round the three central bulbs that had been softened by the remnants of somebody's red shirt-tails.

The bar, on a rickety table by the door, was better stocked underneath than on top. A brimming sheep-trough acted as an ice-bucket.

Although the music made her sad, Tara kept on smiling. She smiled so hard her face ached, and she feared she might be snarling as she tried to talk cheerfully to her friends. But they knew how things were with her, and even their extra kindness made her want to cry.

She couldn't keep her eyes from the door in case Joe came in. This time she had no plan. She stuck to orange-juice and Perrier water because she didn't want to lose control. Balanced on a knife-edge, it wouldn't take much to wobble her off.

'I think it's a group of schoolchildren...'

'Nobody knows exactly where...'

'Trapped on the mountain...'

'Which mountain?'

'The television cameras are'...'Two days, the reporter said to Carl'...'But it's mid-summer'...'These things happen in all weathers'...'When did they leave?'

'What? What are you talking about? Tell me?' Tara felt like Joan of Arc, whirling round following voices, trying to make sense out of half-sentences.

Finally someone acknowledged her and looked down. She was almost pulling at Jeremy's cuffs to get his attention.

'God. You look gorgeous tonight!'

'Jeremy! What's happened?'

'Bit of a drama. Some children are missing from a school-trip up behind Bethesda. No-one knows exactly what happened but the rest of the party turned up this evening with two of their number missing. They'd been searching for them and got lost themselves. The two missing boys have been gone for a day and a night already.'

'And where's Joe?' Afterwards, she didn't know what made her ask. Only that an icy feeling, like quick-moving mercury, tickled her spine and tightened her scalp. '

'He's leading the rescue party...'

'When did he leave?'

Nobody seemed to know. 'When did he leave?' Tara asked them all individually. Eventually somebody said, 'About an hour ago, with Robin.'

Gone to prove himself again, she said to herself angrily as she tore out to the reception hut to try and glean more information. He hasn't learnt his lesson yet! He doesn't need to do any

192

of these things! What is he trying to prove, she sobbed, as she battered her way into the lighted room and tapped on the desk, cursing the height of her heels.

'Yes?' It was the same girl who had talked so glibly about his "wife".

'I'm trying to find out about this mountain accident,' said Tara, keeping a tight control over her rising voice. 'I want to find out where the rescue-party is now. Where would they meet, where would they start from?'

'I can't say.'

'You must say!'

The girl smiled a little nervously. 'No, you've got me wrong,' she said, staring at the bow in Tara's hair, at her crimson dress with its puffy skirt and daring neckline. 'I would tell you but I don't know. Maybe one of the other instructors...it's nothing to do with me, you see...'

The way she said it implied that it didn't have anything to do with Tara, either, and Tara knew that it hadn't. She was being a nosy, interfering member of the public. Perhaps they thought accidents fascinated her...that she was the sort of person who liked to go and watch! This was none of her business at all.

She slammed her way out of reception and made for hut one, but the instructors knew her of old...they were hardly likely to be helpful. A troublemaker, that's what she'd made herself out to be...

'I'm looking for Joe Cornel.' This time she had knocked politely on the door and waited, although in her impatience she twisted her ankles together and wrung her hands.

The mild amusement on Alan's face as he found her on his doorstep brought tears of frustration to her eyes.

'He's not here.' That was Carl's voice from within, but curiosity brought him sauntering to the door to have a look.

'I know he's not here.' Don't upset them, don't rub them up the wrong way by losing your temper, she told herself. 'I know he's gone on the search-party, but I wondered if I could catch him...'

'I don't think he'd want that.' Alan was very serious. 'He's got a job to do and he wouldn't want any diversions...'

'I wouldn't be a diversion! I just need to tell him something.' Couldn't they see how desperate she was? Couldn't they imagine what she must feel like?

'Tell him when he gets back. I'm sure it can wait.'

No, some things just can't wait. But she didn't say it. She knew it would sound foolish, over-excitable, irrational...And she didn't add, what if he doesn't come back, either. The thought was lurking behind her mind like a terrible spectre, as if everything she'd ever dreaded had taken one form and come to haunt her.

'You're not going to help me?' Her voice sounded like a child's.

'I don't think it's a good idea.' Alan's words were final.

'Then I shall find him myself.'

'Wait a minute... Don't be silly...I didn't mean...'

But Tara had gone.

As she wobbled her way along the path to the car-park she could hear the music coming out of the party hut and the odd burst of laughter. It was very dark out here, and very silent. Everything man-made was small and temporary, as fragile as wax candles on the bulk of a birthday-cake, frills and fripperies. The real atmosphere was created by the brooding black mountains and the sloping hillsides,

195

the massive skies and the rushing rivers. She felt extremely small as she scurried towards her car, aware, more than ever before, of her majestic surroundings.

Tara grappled for her torch and turned it on. Even the map fought her, refusing to be spread out properly in the confined space of the Morgan. Where would he go? Where would he go? She studied the ordnance survey map, turning it upside down and round about until it told her what she wanted.

She pushed it aside and started the engine. The headlights and the sound of the engine encapsulated her in a safe little world of her own...but out there it wasn't safe...not at all...especially in the darkness...and Joe was pitting himself against all this might and magnificence, all these powerful forces, an ant on the mountain, yes, that's how small he was.

The road climbed higher and higher, grew narrower and narrower, until it was no more than a track with high grass growing down the middle. The water in the Morgan warned of overheating. Tara ignored it and, keeping her foot on the accelerator, went on climbing. On either side the dry-stone walls became more and more neglected, until they tapered away to nothing, just an odd boulder here and there balanced on its neighbour or standing accusingly alone on the side of the road.

When she saw the lights ahead of her she expected some lonely farmhouse. She would go in and enquire. They'd be bound to know something. She couldn't be lucky enough to have found the place! She had kept going out of a need to do something...a need to go somewhere...after an intelligent appraisal of the map. But the lights were moving. It was not a farmhouse.

She roared to a halt. Several vehicles were parked in the small lay-by that marked the end of the negotiable track. From here on it was walk or go home. She recognised Joe's Range Rover. Her own car lights seemed to caress it as they died.

They seemed to think, at first, that she had something to do with the rescue, because when she asked, 'Where are they?' a man in a duffel coat pointed to some pinpricks of light high up in the distance. It wasn't until she got out of her car that he looked at her curiously and she realised that coming onto a mountain dressed in a crimson ball-gown and satin high heels was not the done thing.

'You'll be cold,' said somebody else kindly, assuming she was a relative. 'Do you want a rug to wrap round you while you wait?'

She told them who she was...a friend of Joe Cornel's she said, and wondered about that afterwards. Would he have described her as that? She gathered they were not climbing, they wouldn't climb at night...they were just covering well-known ground, spread out over the vast area with their lights, calling the names of the boys. The crackling and bleeping of a radio was the only sound up here apart from the dismal moan of the night wind and an occasional observation from the little huddle of people.

There was a specially equipped Land-rover...she saw a couple of stretchers.

Never had time passed so slowly. Tara's heart was in her mouth. Anything could happen to the men out there...one slip...one wrong footing. Even walking in these high mountain ranges was dangerous. The faces of the watchers were patient, patient and resigned, as if they had done this many times before and in far worse conditions than these.

Her eyes watered as she tried to keep them on the firefly lights that moved so slightly in the distant darkness. Sometimes she lost them...and felt ridiculously that she had let Joe down...not even able to do this small thing while he risked his life... Then, undecipherable to her, a message crackled over the airwaves, and the man with the rustling anorak spoke into his handset.

'The boys have been found? Can you confirm that please?'

The boys had been found! Picked up by the police in Bangor, having a whale of a time on a borrowed scooter...drinking under age...

The message was radioed up to the rescue-team.

'Where are you going?'

'They're coming back now, aren't they?'

'Yes, but it'll be some time...'

'That's why I'm going to meet him.'

'Dressed like that?'

Tara had forgotten.

She kicked off her shoes and carried them. Ignoring the amused eyes of the onlookers, she started along the grassy track that led to the shadowy foothills. She had her torch with her, and every now and then her stockinged feet squelched on sheep dirt, but she didn't care. She kept her eyes on the lights. They seemed to pan crazily across the sky as the rescuers made their way back down the mountainside.

Tara walked and walked and walked. Walking in the dark like this, she seemed to be moving in a dreamy time warp...never getting anywhere...the darkness beside her never altering. There were no landmarks, just the far-off gentle shadow changes as the black mass ahead of her spread itself, darkly, to the sky. But the lights ahead grew brighter, came together, and she knew Joe was there somewhere.

Tara Conway didn't care what she looked like or what anyone thought of her. This time she didn't care about making a fool of herself. If he rejected her, then it would be an honest rejection, and she would just have to get over it as best she could. Worse things happened. To go home tomorrow not having said how she felt would be the ultimate betrayal, of herself. And she could fool anyone in any way she liked, but she was never going to fool herself again. Tara had learnt that much.

How many torches were there? They

were all pointed her way. Which was his? Their voices reached her first and even now the shapes of the men were hidden behind a wall of blinding brightness.

'I love you, Joe,' Tara declared in a high treble voice into the mass of brilliance. He was there somewhere. He wasn't going to pass her this time with a dismissive, 'I'll catch you later.'

'I've been stupid.' She stood there, attired like a Christmas fairy, shoes instead of a wand, a battered bow angled crazily in her hair. The lights playing on the shimmering material of her dress blinded her. Her feet were planted squarely on the ground and she held her head high. Her only protection was the arm held up to shield her eyes. 'And I want you to know that I'm sorry. When I thought I might never see you again, I realised I had to be honest, and I want you to be honest, too, Joe.'

She didn't care who else heard her. She didn't care that her hair, so carefully done, had fallen from its clips and stuck to her face in wisps, or that mascara had run down her cheeks following the channels of her tears.

Her breath was coming quickly. This

was the most important moment of her life. She was taking a chance with her new-found self-appreciation. It would have to be strong to survive this sort of exposure. She knew it was. She would never be that helpless little fat person ever again, no matter what Joe said.

He didn't speak. He just came out from behind the wall of light and held her.

The clouds moved off the sky as if some giant teacher was clearing a chalky blackboard. Tara and Joe walked back across the hills by the light of the moon. They didn't need their torches.

In a magic world laced by silver mists, they talked and they kissed as if there was no such day as tomorrow.

'I was so angry with you for coming here tonight,' Tara said. 'I felt you were taking yourself so far away from me...perhaps for ever!'

Shadows played on his face, finding the hollows and contours, illuminating the strength in it. His even teeth glinted in the darkness as he smiled. 'It's something I have to do,' he said. 'Not to prove anything, but just because I like people.'

'Those lost boys didn't sound very likeable to me!'

'You're just jealous!' He squeezed her tightly and she trembled at the strength in his arms. 'As you were when you heard about Anna. You wanted to hurt me as you'd been hurt...and you succeeded!'

'I saw her picture,' she confessed. 'I read your book.'

He didn't seem surprised. 'She's lovely, isn't she?'

When Tara agreed, she felt none of the jealous pangs she'd expected. She understood that their love had died a long time ago, and that that part of Joe's life was over. She didn't need to take anything away from Anna. And yes, she was beautiful.

'But not as beautiful as you are tonight.' He stopped, turned her round and stared down at her, his feelings radiated in his eyes. She touched his face, followed the weathered lines with her fingers, afraid it might go away. She might wake up and find this was a dream, created out of her own need to make this come true.

'I can't believe this is happening to me...and in this place...' Tara breathed in and filled her lungs with intoxicating mountain air. 'Something is bound to happen to spoil it.'

'No.' Joe sounded so certain. 'It can't if we don't let it.'

'I wanted to say...about your book...I wanted to say that I was unhappy, too.'

'I know.' He put his finger over her mouth. 'I knew that when I first saw you. But I had to let you work it out for yourself. Children can be very cruel...'

'So can lots of people.'

'Only if you let them. Not if you feel good here inside.'

'Joe, I love you...and this is only the beginning.' Excitement welled up inside her, fierce and unstoppable as a mountain spring. Tara could hardly contain it. Now, nothing was impossible. Now, she was suddenly alive...and powerful as she'd never felt before. It was all so right! She ran on ahead of him her body light and free! She threw open her arms and shouted out into the darkness, 'I AM SO HAPPY. I AM SO VERY HAPPY!' And the mountains took up the song and relayed it back a hundred times so they were surrounded by echoes of enchanted happiness.

She was shocked when the lights went

on, caught them in the spotlight, and the waiting rescue-party clapped them home.

'I'd forgotten all about...I thought we were alone.' She put her finger shyly to her lips.

'You can go,' Joe told them. 'Just leave us one car in case.'

'In case of what?' asked the man in the duffel coat, smiling.

'In case we ever want to come back,' he said, turning to face the hills, and taking Tara's hand.

When everyone had gone and they were truly alone, he took her in his arms and warmed her. Into the great silence he whispered, 'Trust me,' and she knew that she would do so for the rest of her life.